THE CHOSEN GODDESSES

PORCHES

INDIA · SINGAPORE · MALAYSIA

Copyright © Porches 2024
All Rights Reserved.

ISBN 979-8-89556-972-6

This book has been published with all efforts taken to make the material error-free after the consent of the author. However, the author and the publisher do not assume and hereby disclaim any liability to any party for any loss, damage, or disruption caused by errors or omissions, whether such errors or omissions result from negligence, accident, or any other cause.

While every effort has been made to avoid any mistake or omission, this publication is being sold on the condition and understanding that neither the author nor the publishers or printers would be liable in any manner to any person by reason of any mistake or omission in this publication or for any action taken or omitted to be taken or advice rendered or accepted on the basis of this work. For any defect in printing or binding the publishers will be liable only to replace the defective copy by another copy of this work then available.

Contents

Note From The Author

First up, I sincerely thank you for choosing this book and giving your precious time to read it.

In my first book, "*The Eternal Chaos of Love*," the central theme lies in a phrase that Gautam says to Sana Amyra: "*To love and to be loved is the basic thing one needs in life.*" However, the act of living one's own life path is subjected to various thought processes and lessons that our life teaches us every now and then. Ever since I had published my debut novel, I started researching for an 'idea' that had been in mind for so many seasons. Life's upgrade in terms of mindset and lifestyle helped me to research much further and find a plot to apply the idea that I wanted to narrate through a story, which is my favorite job in life.

I hope this new world, new people, new culture, and new theories will excite you while reading as much as it excited me while I was writing. The entire process, including the designing of the core plot, research, and development, took a nice number of days and months to know the exact ground reality regarding anthropology, geography, and finally the cause and effect that involves belief, love, lust, fundamentals, oppression, gender, sexuality, politics, religion, caste, and everything. I would say I have lived the 18 months of my life with them; I wish and hope you all do after reading this.

Cape Comorin, also known as Kanyakumari, a town that lies at the tip of India, has its own diverse communal and religious versatility. The third biggest tourist attraction in Tamil Nadu not only has some exotic scenic beauties but also some unopened and unspoken communal divergence among the people. I have written some characters in the town only based on local politics and demographic structures and issues relied on that, and there is no intention to degrade or harm anyone's beliefs or practices. This is a work of fiction; any names or characters, businesses or places, or events or incidents are fictitious; any resemblance to actual persons, living or dead, or actual events is purely coincidental.

Tribes are the backbone of the human kind; they are one of the last few traces of evidence left from the ancestors, but today's mechanical world doesn't have any time or care to look back at our roots and take care of them. Several ancient tribal groups have become extinct, and many are about to go extinct without any recognition. Their magical medicinal tactics have played a pivotal role in history.

Kani tribes is one among them in the southern-most tip of Western Ghats at Kerala, near the Agastya Malai. In this fictional story, they are taking the center stage at the village called 'Amboori', a small tribal village in Thiruvananthapuram district. Fictions are always blended with truths; here I have taken the fictional liberty as a license to blend it with the history and its metaphors. The plot, characters, and issues are made fictitious to make it more interesting for the readers. I tried hard and made it blend the true history along with the fictions carefully enough to not to hurt or question any sentiments of any tribal or religious group; however, if anything was mistakenly said or hurt the feelings, I kindly apologize.

In our lives, we have come across many women, starting from our mother, sister, friend, girlfriend, wife, daughter, and granddaughter. We all love them; we care for them, don't we? They have been portrayed as '*Goddesses*' of our lives. At what stage do the fellow humans with the same flesh and blood become our '*deity*'? And at what stage do the same women become '*dirty*'? When does the holiness assert on them? and when does the same retract on them? There might be lots of questions going around.

This novel deals with some goddesses from some religions, like *Goddesses Kumari from Buddhism, Goddesses Athena from Greek, Goddesses Durga from Hinduism, Goddesses Kannagi from Hinduism/Buddhism, and Goddesses Mary Magdalene from Christianity.* There are few characters in this novel who may access the qualities of these goddesses, but who will be the chosen one? To answer this question, fasten your seatbelts and get ready to travel along with me to the southern tip of India.

Love,
Porches

To every woman in my life

Chapter One

"Can we be together forever?" with her head resting on his chest, asked Adina Immaculate in a husky tone, with her half-wavy hair pinned to his shirt buttons. "Hmm" replied Joseph nodding his head in the same husky tone. Bearing all the odds of that late evening wave sound that shatters every pair of ears in Pallam Beach, Kanyakumari, they both heard what they spoke. Joseph slowly eased her hair with his fingers and acted in a way that made her feel more comfortable and confident. Adina suddenly raised her head to look into Joseph's eyes just to gain her confidence and returned to the position immediately.

Adina, a girl in her mid-twenties, was wearing a brown top with slightly pulled-up white leggings, which were partially folded, and her mesmerizing fish-shaped wet eyes were occupied in deep thoughts in the thought of something. Joseph, the same age as Adina, wore a peach-colored t-shirt and blue jeans, a smart watch, was just witnessing the most aesthetic sight of his life, Adina, who was gently resting on his chest. Her brownish-yellow-toned face started to glitter from the evening rays of the sun, that was right above from the sea.

"Why all these odds are happening only for us? Is life that hard?" asked Adina.

Joseph hazed at the beach and saw a crab crawling back to the ocean, he stated, "Adina, life isn't that easy, see look at that crab –" By the time he said this, she closed his mouth with her hands and posted her words,

"Enough of your philosophical classes Joseph. I know what you are going to say and believe me when I say this is the nth time I'm listening to this crab philosophy, at the same beach, all the time! Aren't you bored?" Finally, her husky voice mingled with emotions and said goodbye and a loud voice popped up.

"I'm too fed up with your blabbering, Adina. We are here to chill, and it has been a while since we hung out. Thankfully you took a leave today, otherwise, our not-seen-streak would be still going on, uh?" Joseph slightly lashed out at Adina.

Suddenly she got up and gave a mighty stare at him and cleaned the beach sands from her dress and walked towards the waves, furiously. She turned back to Joseph who was still sitting in the same place. Then she ran towards him splashing the water from her bottle onto his face making him sprint up from where he was sitting. Immediately, she started running and he chased her.

The couples revolved around the beach for quite some time, chasing each other and playing with sand. At one point, she stopped near the shore right where she was. The ice-cooled somewhere-between-evening-and-night waves hit her legs. She didn't realize that as she was so busy staring at the sea and the sky. He slowly came near her and whispered in her ears,

"The Sun is going to set now, do you believe it will come back?"

She nodded her head denoting yes, and Joseph asked "How come you say this with much confidence?"

"You're are nuts; it is the universal truth and it's never going to change"

"Hmm, we'll be together forever; that is also a universal truth and it's never going to change", said Joseph.

Suddenly her face changed slightly and she looked into the eyes of Joseph for a few seconds and mouthed "Love you". Immediately, he recognized it but he acted in a way that he was unable to understand and kept asking her to say it loudly but she was hesitant and that made her blush. At that time, she received a call from her mother, and at once, her calm and happy face grew anxious and she told Joseph, "It's time we left".

"Why did that Sun set much sooner today?" said Joseph in a sad tone.

They both came back to the road from the shore. Adina helped Joseph to clear the tangles of his messy hair, as he always had thin hair which is prone to get unaligned. Eventually, she got ready to get back home as well. He hit the engine and the couple started the ride.

In the middle of the ride, he asked, "Adina, shall we get back my camera from the rent? It's already a day-long"

"Jo, do you think we have time? My mom called me twice, I need to call back only after getting on the bus, I'm already tensed," replied Adina.

He remained silent and drove the bike pulling a long face, thinking about his camera which is his asset. He was working as a professional photographer in the town, he was best known for the aesthetic frames that he captured. He was one of the prominent photographers in the town. He had an office in the Ransom town area and a branch office near Kanyakumari railway station, which was being managed by his friend. He owned three high-end costly cameras which he bought through a bank loan. He gave one of them, to a foreigner that morning, in exchange for his passport as a caution deposit.

Thinking about his camera and how far it stayed away from him, his face changed completely.

She saw his face through the rear mirror and tapped him on his shoulder and said, "Let's go and get the camera but please don't keep your face as if I'm kidnapping you".

"Really, which kidnapper sits like a queen and lets the victim drive the bike?" he asked.

"Where is he?" she queried. Joseph stopped his bike and called to contact him whom he saved as "Brandon".

"Brandon, where are you? It's been a day already. By now you would have captured two sunsets and a sunrise," he said over the call.

"Hey, mate! I'm here, umm well near the beach, near the Gandhi memorial," said Brandon over the phone.

Joseph hung up the call after acknowledging him and looked at Adina, who signaled with her hands to go ahead.

They reached the place that was jammed with traffic and crowds, surrounded by so many tourists. Amidst that cramped place, minutes later, they were able to find Brandon, a trippy white guy from Australia who wore a sleeveless t-shirt showing all his weird tattoos on his arms. He waved at them and gave the camera back to him.

"Man, wanna join our late evening party tonight at our place? Come as my guest to Fox Hotels. My girls are coming over, and also they got some awesome liquors out there. Wanna join us and chill?," he asked Joseph. He immediately turned back at Adina and looked anxiously but with a smile.

"Buddie, I'm running late. Why don't you text me later? See you soon, bye," said Joseph and rode away.

"See you soon" she mimicked him and said, "I know why you wanna join him and party? Because of the girls right?"

"Adi, I have his passport, and it was out of courtesy that he called. Do you think I will go leaving all my work? Do you remember? We planned to meet here every morning just to make our day better. That's a good plan, right? How can I miss that," said Joseph. She remained silent and they reached the bus stand.

Before boarding the Anjugramam bus from the Kanyakumari bus stand, she frowned and stared at him which had a thousand meanings that only Joseph knew.

As soon as she got on the bus, she called her mom,

"Ma, I'll be home in half an hour," she let her mother know.

"It's already 7, how long will you work in a day?" asked her mom over the phone.

Adina felt a bit guilty as she lied to her mom that she was working, but took a day off just to spend time with Joseph.

He saw her from the bike until the bus disappeared from the bus stand and he slowly rode the bike across the road as the bus passed by. Suddenly a black Scorpio car crossed across almost hitting Joseph.

In the wink of an eye, he turned in shock to look who that was and started cussing at whoever was in the car. Within seconds, a small crowd gathered near Joseph and examined the situation looking at the car.

The man inside the car was in his late twenties, looked furiously at Joseph and the crowd with his phone in his ears. He wore a heavy gold chain with a crucified cross pendant, a plain white shirt with a clumsy beard and mustache, and black pants. He opened the door, stepped on the road, and looked at Joseph. Quickly after, murmurs started to spread to the surrounding area. A hand from the car pulled him by calling, "Durai…Durai…get inside soon", and he got inside the car.

"Look we're just about to clear a case, and you are under surveillance by the cops. Please be silent, we have some important work to do" said the Lawyer Gopal, who was sitting in the back seat, with the same outfit as Durai.

Peter Durai, a short-term local goon who is upcoming as the next biggest goon in the town, wanted to be the head of the cape and rule the town having his only community as his whole strength. He glared at Joseph once again when the car crossed his bike. He then continued his conversation over the phone.

"Peter Durai…Peter Durai…" the person over the phone kept calling him.

"Yes," he blurted out in anger.

"It is not my fault to get myself transferred. Who would love to vacate the homeland and be here somewhere that is completely foreign? It was all because of you. You killed, you murdered people and I had to support you as a cop, Huh? What would that make of me? A transfer is the very last thing I got as the SP is our community man." said the transferred Deputy Superintendent of Police, Murugan over the phone.

"Fuck, it is not because of me. You cannot work things out. My bad I believed you just because you are from my community. Do you know what that fucking bastard did? He wanted a girl from our cas…anyway who is coming here as the new DySP" Peter fumed back at Murugan.

"Arockiyaraj Fernandez, from Devakottai, Ramnad district," Murugan replied.

"Who is he, is he…?" he asked.

"No…" he said.

Peter immediately hung up the call and tapped his head back at the seat in anger. Lawyer Gopal tried to calm him down by saying,

"Let us ask him. Let me take care of him and you won't be worried"

Meanwhile, Joseph reached his office at Ransom Town and kept the camera. He received a call from Brandon.

"Dude, are you joining?" he asked in a cherishing voice.

Joseph's face changed slightly and sighed over the phone which Brandon heard. He realized that this would bring up issues with Adina but still, the inner part of his mind wanted to party hard. Suddenly, he received a call from his mom. He asked Brandon to hold the call and answered his mother's,

"Joseph, are you done?" asked his mom Jesintha, over the phone, who was in church, wearing a sari, in a way her pallu covered her head. She worked as a government school teacher and she used to attend almost all masses conducted by their local church in Arokiyapuram.

"Ma, I'll be home in half an hour" he replied.

"Oh, I'm sorry Joseph, I just came to church for the evening "peace be with you" mass, and I thought that you would come late as usual. So are you coming here for mass? We'll get back home together?" asked his mom.

Joseph's face shattered in discomfort, as he was not a guy who liked to attend church masses, so he immediately asked his mom to hold the call and retrieved Brandon's and said,

"Dude, I'm coming, make space for me," he said in a hurry and cut the call.

"Ma, please get back home soon, have dinner, and take your medicines. I'll be coming in the morning. I have a shoot that came up just now. Please understand ma," he rushed not allowing his mom to reply as he knew that she would be thrashing him anyway. She called again and he answered,

"Ma, I know, you will scold me but this is my nature of work, you have to understand."

His mom interrupted, "Joseph…."

"Ma, please this is the only thing I ask you now," he shouted.

"But, Joseph listen to me…," again his mom interrupted which only triggered him to shout again.

In reply, his mom yelled which made her neighbor lady in the church go mad and she also shushed her "aaargh" out of fear. The father noticed it and said in common, "Peace be with you,".

Her neighbor lady also joined and said "Teacher, Peace be with you."

Joseph asked over the phone, "Okay ma, what were you about to tell?"

His mom who was still in embarrassment, said "Peace be with you."

Joseph smiled, cut the call, and called his close friend, Zayan,

"Asalamu alaikum," said his friend.

"Shu… I know you would be sleepy, finish the Iftar and come to my office. Hand over the albums to a client and finish the unfinished projects dot mp4 and dot jpegs right now, okay?"

"Hello, I'm still in bed man, you forgot? This is a Ramzan month, I didn't even complete fasting prayer and I need to go the Mosque and…." Joseph hung up the call immediately.

When Adina reached her house in Anjugramam, she came in to see her father, Christopher Raj, wearing a t-shirt and lungi, watching a political debate show about Indian economics. She saw him and didn't speak anything and went inside. Her mom, Evangeline Mary was in the kitchen. Adina entered her room, changed her dress, and she heard her father's voice.

"Tell her not to over work, overtimes aren't good. Her health is not as important as the society, tell her to be safe and secure," her father said to his wife.

Adina listened to everything and remembered her father's words when she joined the design field first. He panicked a lot about the software industry but only for Adina's wish, he accepted her to work that too in the town, though she had better offers in other big cities.

She was called by her mom for dinner. She also called out,

"Abraham…Abraham…," and shouted for a long time. A man with curly hair, wearing a T-shirt came out of a room holding a phone in his hand. Abraham, the younger brother of Adina who just finished college and currently studying a crash course on coding for his father's sake.

"Ma, what's wrong with you? I have some work to do," Abraham lashed out at his mom, and his father from the hall turned to look at him. Immediately, he went to the dining table. All four members of the family were present at the dining table.

Pre-food prayers were said and all four began to eat. Abraham was completely occupied with his mobile, which Adina noticed and gestured a warning through her eyes, to keep his phone aside. But he didn't care about her. Suddenly, she was reminded of her boyfriend Joseph. So, she took her phone and texted him, but she didn't receive a quick reply. She soon finished her chapattis and went inside the room to call him.

She called him.

"Sorry," said Joseph.

"I know you wouldn't miss the party, I hate you," said Adina.

"Adina…Adina…please listen! I was about to go home but my mom is still in church. Where would I go?" he asked on a lighter note.

"Don't you have a key?" she asked furiously.

"Yes, I do have but my mom doesn't know," he pulled down his voice.

"Enough of your reasoning. Just tell me how many girls?" she asked in the same tone.

"Only one. There are not many girls and I think he cheated me, that too the close friend of our Brandon," he said, and Brandon said a big "yes" from behind.

"She's Alyssa from Australia, she's cool as well having similar tattoos as Brandon. She has the coolest studs and septum, is nicely dressed, and is also a blonde," he said in a half-drunken state holding a beer in his hand.

Adina's eyes lit up and asked, "Are you going home tonight?"

"Big No. I cannot go home drunk Adi, I'll be caught red-handed," he replied.

"Jo, you're going off your limits. I feel its is not right to stay with them," Adina said calmly.

"You don't believe me, uh? Believe me, I'm gonna share the room with Brandon, not with any girl, especially Alyssa, believe girl."

"Do whatever you want, but don't miss turning up in the morning," she said before hanging up the call. She went to bed.

The next morning, she woke up, had breakfast, and got ready for the office.

She reached the Kanyakumari bus stand and waited some time for Joseph but he didn't turn up. She called him several times, but he didn't pick up. She got scared then and went to Fox Hotels to check on him. She asked about Brandon and knocked on his room.

Brandon opened, and Adina sneaked a glance into his room but she couldn't find Joseph.

"Are you searching for Joseph?" he asked and she nodded.

He guided her to the next room and knocked twice. Alyssa opened the door and eventually, Adina sneaked into her room.

Joseph was asleep on the bed and he was hungover.

She fell in shock and started crying. Joseph woke up in a few seconds and greeted Adina casually. It took him seconds to realize what was going on. He saw her crying and got up from bed.

Adina didn't seem to be okay and strode away from that place. Joseph ran behind her in the streets and almost reached the Kanyakumari bus stand.

"Adina, please listen, there is nothing to cry about," he tried to soothe her.

Suddenly Adina stopped, turned at him, and said "Nothing? This is nothing? Okay, it's going to be nothing from now on between us, it's over...over."

Joseph closed his eyes in frustration and she had already walked a long way enough to disappear from his sight.

Chapter Two

When things got messed up in Kanyakumari between Adina and Joseph, things were even worse in the village of Amboori, a mountain village located approximately eighty kilometers from the cape of India, in Kattakadu Taluk of Thiruvananthapuram district, Kerala state. It is located in the southernmost district of Kerala. Amboori village is one of the ending points of the Western Ghats and is surrounded by Neyyar Wildlife Sanctuary in the east, Kallikadu in the west, Aryan code in the southwest, and Vellarada in the south. The divine beauty of Kerala's Western Ghats ends here.

In that village, a rock named Dravyapara is situated and besides that, there is an ethnic tribal group called 'Kanikars" living for thousands of years, in fact ever since mankind's evolution happened in this part of the world. The oldest group has around five hundred members in the region. The rock has more mythical histories spanning from almost five thousand years ago.

Dravyapara is known in mythical history as the loan-lending rock. It is said that in those times, the poor people of Amboori used to request loans from an anonymous goddess in the Dravyapara rock. People used to shout louder near the granite door at the northeastern part of the rock. Once, the goddess approves the loan, the southeastern part of the rock has one granite bucket where the requested loan amount will be filled. The same bucket will be used to repay the loan amount and should be shouted aloud as the loan money is deposited. It was an unwritten rule that no one should sneak inside the door.

Some hundred years ago, a man named Kadamban climbed up to the rock and asked for some amount of money to travel to various places to sell the honey he extracted. He climbed and shouted aloud at the northeastern granite gate and looked up at the sky. He felt a bit divine and realized the clouds were moving fast and immediately he listened to the sound of golden coins pouring into the bucket at the southeastern part. He resisted himself not to look at that side as no one should see inside that granite door. When the place was noiseless, he slowly went to the granite bucket and he was very happy to see the money he requested. He confidently gave assurance to repay once he sold all the honey he had.

Kadamban sold all the honey to various parts but still, he couldn't repay the money he bought as a loan. Days, months, and years passed, and gradually, the honey extracted by Kadamban's family hit a huge amount. So one day his son decided to repay the loan his father bought. He went to Dravyapara and deposited the money and shouted aloud but he got curious to see who the money lender was, and so he decided to see inside the rock, which is forbidden in their culture.

He slowly went near the granite door and waited for someone to come and collect the money. After waiting for some time, he heard someone coming out and he was so excited. Soon he was shocked to see a beautiful naked woman coming out of the rock, collecting the money, and returning. He watched her, admired her beauty, and was mesmerized by her beauty. Suddenly the nude woman noticed him and instantly a large thunderclap occurred, the gate closed immediately, and it never opened again until today.

Since then, the people of that village have been practicing ritual worship at the southeastern granite gate to calm down the goddess and hope to see that gate open again. Several festivals were organized by the villagers including Sasthan festival along with Vadamala boothan's pooja, which was believed to be done to calm down the ghost creature that lives beyond the Dravyapara which is acting as a guardian for the village's agriculture crop to sow and reap. Most of the time they believed in the dedication to the nude woman that was believed to live inside Dravyapara. Thereafter, some of the women in that village fasted and set their bodies clean without having sex for seven days if they were married, and came in nude to Dravyapara and did rituals for the good sake of their village. Some villagers said that the goddess once turned up and said "I will open the door on the day you sow and reap the rice in one single day", so the Kanikars took agriculture seriously and consistently cultivated the fields without fail alongside their traditional occupation of honey extraction.

*   *   *

At present, one fine rainy day, a few villagers lifted an old woman who was sitting on a chair that was placed on a cot. The woman on the chair was Isabella, who was then one hundred and seventeen years old and the oldest surviving person in that village, also in the entire Kanikar tribe. She was covered with a sack on her head just to get rid of drizzles sliding on her wrinkle-filled face and she was wearing a cotton sari with a blouse her hair which once was as dark as a raven then turned into a creamy white. She was taken to the southern part of Dravyapara Rock and was made to sit in front of it for rituals. She was offered sweets and fruits and she ate those even though she was completely toothless.

She was not only the oldest woman living in the village but also the weirdest woman in the village. She was a half-Christian and half-Hindu. She used to talk to herself but also spat facts at times regarding the important events and decisions of the Kanikar tribe. They treated her like a Godmother. She had one weirdest belief that Lord Krishna from Hinduism and Jesus Christ from Christianity were the same. She got confused with both gods at one stage and still hadn't recovered from that state of Trance. She also acted weirdly concerning sunrise and sunsets, she loved those times and she believed and worshiped Lord Krishna when the sun stayed in the east and started worshiping Jesus Christ when the sun comes to the west.

Some villagers took her to the gate and made ritual worship to make the goddess open the door. Isabella was sitting calmly witnessing everything. As it started to rain cats and dogs, she was taken to a shelter nearby, and the people continued the rituals.

However, that rainy day was not a fine day for one family as their oldest member, a man named Parapan, died, who was one hundred-and-one-year-old who lived through a century. The day was sad, and they announced his death through phone calls as usual to their distant relatives, and also the neighbors came to know it owing to the unusual happenings from Parapan's house. Even though the death news had spread throughout the entire village despite the heavy rain, his family members were determined to fulfill their traditional way of declaring his death in a proper way. So, they called for a man who usually makes public announcements, especially. death.

The drummer named Maadan started announcing the death of Parapan. He had seventeen grandchildren and nine children with the four wives he had. The news spread across Dravyapara where the ritual worship was taking place. On hearing this news, Isabella immediately laughed and said,

"Bloody! He won. We had a bet! Who would go first? He made a bet that if he died first then he'll offer me a tender coconut with pure honey. I guess he might bring me one tonight."

Everyone surrounding her looked at Isabella once and resumed their ritual.

"He was a womanizer. Such a man he was back in our days. He was sixteen years younger than me, but still hit on me. Little kiddo of my time. Anyway Praise the Lord Jesus, may his soul rest in peace, and I need to be present at Selvam's daughter's wedding. Please finish the work quickly," Isabella said and no one cared about her blabbering and continued their work.

Two women were talking about Selvam's daughter's marriage and that they couldn't find a garland for the bride, as the bridegroom didn't arrange it properly. Isabella, who holding the sack to cover her head from raindrops, listened to this.

Maadan went to various streets, and when he entered Chithirai Street, he drummed and announced the death of Parapan as he was one of the most respectful persons in the village. In Chithirai Street, a man, in a green-painted house, was seen shaping his mustache with a mirror in front of him, stopped his work and listened to that announcement. He immediately came out and paid keen attention to the announcement. He immediately shouted a name,

"Mullaa..."

Mulla a short man with a towel on his shoulders came and asked, "What happened?"

"It is Parapan. He had all the privileges in the village. We should be the ones to pay the respect first and show who we are in this village, I need to be the next Moothakaani at least by this year, Mulla.... Get the garland ready, we must do the respect before him," he said.

The man himself went by the name Maarthandan. He was one of the stalwarts of the Kanikar tribes in the Amboori village. He was in contention of becoming a Mootakani a prestigious post of the village. It had all the authorities including decisions being made. But he was not the only one in the line.

As Maadan passed through Aavani Street, there was one house built in the wood where a man was sitting and tearing a jack fruit, delivering all his strength alongside the children.

Meanwhile, he listened to the news bearer, and he immediately withdrew, letting go all his strength from the jackfruit making the kids around him fall with force. He showed interest in respecting Parapan as it would help him score better than Marthandan in the race for Moothakani.

"Valli…"

"I heard the news, the garland with flowers was ordered already Mullan who is climbing above here in a bike from Vellarada. You don't worry Kaliyan", said Valli, a thirty-year-old woman in his house, who took care of the few children in the place built by Kaliyan.

This man is Kaliyan, who was also in the race for the Moothakani post.

To earn the Moothakani post, Isabella had to choose one among the people of Kanikar with quite a brave record. It would be assigned through the voting system of the people, between two or three candidates who opted to serve the tribal needs and also to establish their tribal essence, advancing the lifestyle of Kanikars.

That day, the entire village seemed to be quite busy as one of the respectable businessmen in Kanikar named, Selvam had arranged a marriage for his daughter on the very same day. This man used to export honey abroad, which the Kanikar people extracted. Parapan's death shook the village and the entire village was looking for flowers and garlands to pay last respects to Parapan.

Almost half of the village collected flowers from their backyard and some got from the limited shop in that village.

Meanwhile, Kaliyan was washing his hands to get rid of the oil he had applied to cut jackfruit earlier. He remembered the marriage in Selvam's house. He wanted to attend as Selvam held a good name in the village, and he wanted to respect him with a gesture by attending his daughter's marriage. He thought this would gain momentum alongside him to become the Moothakani.

The same was thought by Marthandan who was said to be the arch-rival of Kaliyan,

"Parapan's death – Selvam's daughter's marriage! I guess it is the time to kill two birds with one stone," said Marthandan with a cigarette in his hand.

"Marthandan, no flowers are left in the village because of the heavy rain over the past three days. It's Madan who has bought flowers and garland from Vellarada. He was climbing up the hill on a bike and we had to wait for him," said Mullan.

Marthandan put down the cigarette, rubbed it with his toes, and asked Mullan to start their old jeep to Parapan's house.

Marthandan, a forty-five-year-old man with salt and pepper colored hair and the same-colored beard in a clumsy pattern, an unshaped body wearing a brown shirt and white dhoti, took the front seat in the jeep and reached Parapan's house without any garlands. Parapan's house was located on a slope as the road cutting his house tangentially is a great slope. People used to walk with a bit of extra effort.

He entered the house, saw all those loud crying women, entered inside, and was shocked to see Kaliyan sitting inside before him.

Kaliyan, a forty-five-year-old man with hair that was well groomed and a salt and pepper beard with proper texture, wore a black shirt and a brown dhoti and was sitting on a chair with one leg over the other.

Parapan's family members placed the chair beside Kaliyan for Marthandan, first Marthandan hesitated and then took that seat.

Meanwhile, Madan called Valli, who was sitting nearer to Kaliyan. She attended the call to hear, "Valli, I'm stuck here, my bike is dry without fuel, and it is raining heavily here. I can't climb up here. I think I'm unable to reach up there within today," said Madan over the phone. Valli cut the call and let Kaliyan know. Marthandan also listened to it and planned for something else.

Meanwhile, at Selvam's daughter's marriage, the shortage of flowers also affected the scenario. His daughter, twenty-three-year-old Lakshmi was waiting inside the room for the garland to arrive for her marriage. Selvam a renowned big shot in that community was left without any flowers for his daughter's marriage.

At the funeral house, where the corpse was placed to pay respect, only a few came with flowers, plucked from the trees roadside and also from the border forest area nearby. At that time a woman in her forties wearing a white sari and cross dollar chain on her neck with cleanly combed oily hair, holding a small ring of flowers and then placing that ring on Parapan's body, paid her last respect. An old lady from the crowd asked that woman, "Melisa, where are these flowers from?"

"From the feet of Jesus Christ," said Melisa, a nun in that village who worked in and for the church and also served as a social worker regarding Kanikar community problems. She also seemed to be upset about the shortage of flowers due to southwest monsoon rain in the recent past. Another old lady got up from the crowd and blessed Melissa saying "Praise the Lord, May the shepherd be watching everything."

Marthandan's face changed slightly on seeing Melissa and he pretended that he didn't see her. Kaliyan noticed Marthandan's face change and looked at Valli. Suddenly, Marthandan stood up and said,

"What's up with all the ruckus here? Who the hell is he? He is Parapan, and he served our community for the all years he lived. There is still honey left in his bag. we should be sending him with all dignity and respect, but look we are here without flowers". He shouted at the crowd and sat back as no one responded seriously to the commotion he raised.

Kaliyan giggled subtly and Marthandan noticed that, and frowned at him.

Rain got even heavier and the sound of thunderstorms was raising the tension of the situation.

Meanwhile, the rituals at Dravyapara ended in heavy rain, and the offerings were served to Isabella before she was taken to the funeral.

"Let me see the kiddo Parapan one last time," said Isabella.

Meanwhile, Mullan received a call from Selvam's house and a man spoke over the phone, "Mullan, do you know anyone who could get into the forest in this heavy rain? Lakshmi needs a garland for her marriage?'

"Are you kidding? Do you know what the weather is? It is very hard even for a corpse now to get a flower and you are asking for a bride?" said Mullan furiously.

"Eda, Mulla! You know how hard the situation here is. It is not possible and good for the bride to get married without a single garland. Will they see it as a good sign, listen, this is time for Marthandan to get a good name with Selvam. Please ask him to find a solution," said the man over the phone.

Marthandan saw Mullan's face and asked "What?"

Mullan hesitated and continued over the phone, "What solution, do you want him to pluck a garland from the dead body and lay it on the couple?"

Both Marthandan and Kaliyan looked at Mullan who was losing his mind over the phone.

Then, the relatives of Parapan announced that the body would be taken for the funeral. Suddenly an old man came running, fully drenched in rain, and was holding a garland in his hand. The entire crowd stood stunned looking at this garland.

"My dear friend, I thought you would see another Sasthan festival, Vadamala bootham will miss you my friend Parapan," the old man cried holding the garland in his hand.

Both Marthandan and Kaliyan stared at the garland, and Marthandan stood up and asked that old man to stop crying and said,

"Enough, Parapan will attain peace. Now please stop crying and take a rest or else you will find a seat alongside Parapan. Give me the garland, I'll take care"

"This is not fair, is it? I came before him now look he is grabbing the garland from that pitiful old man," Kaliyan stood up and shouted at the crowd.

"Please ask him to stop talking rubbish," said Marthandan to the crowd again.

"Eda, who's talking rubbish. I'm the one who came first to pay respect to Parapan. Just look at your dirty beard and uncombed hair. Do you want to be in front of the crowd, Mayire?" said Kaliyan,

As he used the bad word "Mayire" in both Tamil and Malayalam, Marthandan got frustrated and immediately he slapped in his unique way as he always got booth his hands criss cross tightly and release it freely to gain the full thrust and Kaliyan who shook by this, gained courage and slapped him back at Marthandan.

Valli and Mullan tried to stop them but they didn't care. They started to wrestle. Melissa didn't care about their fight and she simply watched them calmly.

They both got involved in a serious fight. As they got off the house and headed to the sloping road, they both slipped together, and they both rolled on the wretched road in that heavy rain. The only garland left in that village was also spoiled in between their fight and they both got fully wet. They were stopped by a group of people and realized they that they were acting out of anger and noticed Isabella was sitting on the top of the chariot kind of cot they carried. They both stood up and greeted Isabella together with respect.

Slowly the sun set, and the darkness slowly surrounded Amboori earlier due to gloomy clouds.

"Lord Krishna, may these little kids be with you," she said and asked her crew to get her down, and was guided to Parapan's house.

She looked at Parapan's corpse for a few seconds and said, "Don't forget our deal, and come back with tender coconut and honey". She suddenly took a garland from the dead body and started going away. Everyone stood in silence watching Isabela do that.

She asked her crew to take her to Selvam's daughter's village immediately,

The crew put down the chariot-like cot and asked to hire an auto as the ritual ended at the moment when Isabela stepped down from the cot.

She was taken in an auto to Selvam's daughter's marriage with a garland from Parapan's corpse.

She entered the marriage hall with huge respect from the people gathered there. She saw Selvam sitting frustrated and called him,

"What's wrong with the bridegroom? Why didn't he respond to this situation?" she asked.

"I don't know ma, I think they are too frustrated to act," said Selvam in a polite manner.

She saw the bridegroom Madhesh with a pitty face and slowly walked towards Lakshmi, the bride and put the garland on her neck, and asked them to get married. Selvam was satisfied and the marriage hall came back to life.

Isabella sat in the chair with her crew members, and Mani, one of the young members of the ritual crew asked, "Ma, what have you done? You took a garland from a corpse and put it on a bride, don't you feel anything?"

She looked at him and looked at the wedding stage, where Lakshmi and her bridegroom were sitting, and smiled.

"Ask both Marthandan and Kaliyan to meet me tomorrow morning."

Chapter Three

Meanwhile, in Cape Comorin, the sad waves spread equally between Joseph and Adina. On the other hand, a newly appointed police inspector, MR. Arockiyaraj Fernandez got ready for his first day as Deputy Superintendent of Police Kanyakumari.

Arockiyaraj was keenly adjusting his mustache with a sharp scissor keeping his face very near to the mirror. He then adjusted his hair a bit and wore his newly ironed rough khaki uniform, which had three stars on the shoulder along with his name badge. He saw a jeep coming to his doorstep and he came out to see a lot of policemen getting ready for their work in the police quarters. He got in the jeep and asked the driver to reach the Deputy Superindetnted office quickly.

They crossed the Kanahapuram signal where they could see the traffic police who were checking the school students and stopping the cycles of the school students.

Arockiyaraj asked his driver about this,

"What is wrong with them? Why are they checking the school students' cycles? Are they supposed to have any license here?"

"Sir, it is not about license sir. It is cannabis checking. The students are more addicted to these than the regular alcohol and smoking sir, it is common here, especially among teenage boys sir," said the driver.

Arockiyaraj closely looked at those boys who were standing for the checking.

They reached the circle office to join as the DySP of Kanyakumari town circle,

He went into his cabin to see all the flower bouquets along with greetings for his transfer.

"Can you please make circle inspectors meet me?" asked DySP Arockiyaraj as the very first query after taking charge.

Immediately all Circle Inspectors reached his room as they were waiting to greet them.

"What's so hot in the town?" asked Arockiyaraj.

"Yeah sir, it's near to the equator as you know it, Kanyakumari is always hotter sir," said one of the Circle Inspectors.

"No, I asked about the hot crimes and cases to be noted," Arockiyaraj asked in a very polite way. At that time, he started reading the greetings he received on his table.

One of the Circle Inspectors began.

"Sir, here in Kanyakumari there are three castes that are prominent among the people, which is irrespective of their religion. Most of them are Christians. They converted their religion but not their caste. Each has its gang and every gang is shaped into an association and every association has its own leader, under whom most of their community members act and obey their orders,"

"Orders? In which sense?" asked Arockiyaraj.

"Sir, among those three prominent castes, one is considered as low caste like untouchables historically deriving from Hindu mythology they say. They are treated as untouchables still. One of the major problems here is the honor killing. There have been around seventy honor killing cases filed in our circle in the past six months. This is only the recorded one which is not even one-third of the actual events that occurred and a very cruel incident took place just a week ago near Aralvamozhi. In fact, that particular case was the reason why the previous DySP to transf –" Arockiyaraj stopped him and said,

" 'Aralvaimozhi, Nandhini case', the girl was blindfolded in front of some men and she was brutally killed by them, pity that the girl never knew who killed her, I suppose it may be her father, the honor killing!" and he asked someone else to speak.

The other cop started, "Sir not only the caste crisis, but there is also another major issue happening around the town. It is cannabis…it revolves around the students predominantly, they are addicted to it completely and that leads to so many anti-social activities sir. This needs to be sto –" Again Arockiyaraj stopped them and in the meantime, he read all the greetings he received.

"So I need those two men who are responsible for these two anti-social elements, that is honor killing and the other one is Cannabis…get them immediately," asked Arockiyaraj.

All the cops standing before him murmured among themselves and Arockiyaraj looked at them.

Suddenly a cop said, "Sir, it is not about two men. Only one person is responsible for both."

"Who is he?" asked Arockiyaraj.

"Peter Durai is a short-term gangster who has his own caste background. He initiated his own caste association and he managed it. He also helps in lending men to safeguard his caste and community members and also helps them in honor killing at the same time he earns great money by selling these cannabis and weeds through his men…" said a cop.

"Where is he?" asked Arockiyaraj calmly.

"Sir, after the case he absconded, now our circle is searching for him, but without proper evidence sir, but also sir, it seems like he did kill the girl Nandhini at Aralvaimozhi in such a cruel way" said the other cop.

"Ahem, okay alright don't worry, the most wanted criminal will meet me and he will reach me very soon and until then you guys…stay tuned and have a party," said Arockiyaraj with a smiling face.

✷ ✷ ✷

Meanwhile, with all these happening at the other corner of the town, Joseph rested his head on his office table and sadly scrolled the mobile screen. Every now and then, he called Adina, but she didn't respond to his call. Then he decided to go home, packed the things, and started the bike. He received a call from Brandon, but he didn't attend. He drove to his home. He was welcomed by his mom with a piece of cake and chips that he bought the other night. He got refreshed and tried to call Adina who kept ignoring his call. She was upset and couldn't concentrate on her work as she was crying in the bathroom, ignoring his calls.

Joseph didn't have any food and he continuously received calls from Brandon and Alyssa. At the same time, his mom was waiting outside his room with the lunch for him. He answered the call at one point and said, "Please leave me alone, it's already messed up here"

"That's why I called you. I reckon you should sit and talk with her and explain what this shit is all about," said Brandon.

"Exactly, the shit it is," replied Joseph.

"I mean that's not really shit. You should have to watch your words, mate," said Alyssa furiously.

"It is all because of you, every damn thing…" Joseph hung up the call even before he was finished with his sentence.

His Mom Jesintha was watching him shouting at someone and moved away. Joseph again called Adina. This time Adina attended the call and said, "See, there is nothing to talk about here. You're a born cheater."

"Okay, at least give me a chance to prove why I cheated. Please wait at our place, Adina, it can't be over like this, I never expected this to happen" said Joseph.

"Even I didn't," Adina said in her shaking voice and cut the call.

Joseph shook his head and called Brandon,

"Four thirty at the bus stand, please assemble along with Alyssa," said Joseph.

"Okay, so today are you in for a party?" he asked.

Joseph left in silence.

❋ ❋ ❋

At four thirty at the bus stand, Joseph waited for Adina while biting his nails as if his nails would go extinct sooner. Both Brandon and Alyssa came to the spot and greeted Joseph with a warm smile. Joseph didn't smile back but gave them a weird stare.

Suddenly the town bus arrived. Adina got down from the bus slowly beyond the excessive crowd from the bus. Her wavy hair shone bright courtesy of yellowish sunshine. Joseph smiled at her and she didn't respond to him. Brandon giggled with Alyssa and Joseph warned him to keep quiet.

"I have to go, please don't make a scene and make me cry here in public," she said in a soft voice.

"I know I'm the culprit, and culprits are never allowed to talk, let them speak" replied Joseph.

"Wait…wait…wait…can you guys just tell me what's the real problem here? I mean, yeah, Joseph told me…I can explain, but what I need to know is, do you guys love each other?" asked Brandon. Neither Joseph nor Adina uttered a word.

"Okay, it's time to open up, Adina, you need to know about something called "hook-ups", it is not actually a casual date or a relationship, it is slightly close to a one-night stand but I reckon it is not. It is all about two people meeting somewhere, which may be a bar, hotel, theatre, or maybe online, they go together for a night and have random sex, that is how the world works now, and you should have to accept it Adina, it is…in fact, it was a great night," said Brandon and Alyssa was looking at him without a word.

Adina's eyes started to work up, and she started feeling uncomfortable being there and walked away. Immediately Joseph patted his forehead in frustration as Brandon increased the tension there.

Alyssa who was silently watching all these, pulled Brandon back and rushed towards Adina, stopped her, and said,

"Please stop crying…You're looking like a brave girl, what made you piss off? Do you think Joseph hooked up with me last night? Definitely not."

Adina's eyes didn't stop from pouring tear droplets in regular periods.

"Girl, I know you can't get my words, it is simple, I can't hook up with someone like Joseph…" said Alyssa.

Adina slowly raised her pupil toward Alyssa.

"Yeah, I'm into girls. I'm a lesbian and I won't be hooking up with men and that guy Brandon, and he is gay. We're queer." Alyssa said and held her hands.

Adina's face changed drastically into a confused state.

"Brandon actually hooked up with a man last night, so Joseph and I stayed together in a room leaving Brandon alone. Joseph and I talked a lot, we were laughing for so many hours, and it had been so long since I met a straight male. He was nice, and guess what he was talking about?" she paused and looked at her eyes for a second and said "These eyes."

✳　✳　✳

"Alyssa, you should know about a girl who gave everything for me and gained nothing for her... You should know about a girl, who walked away from the class just because I was ill-treated there... You must know about a girl who rushed two hundred kilometers to check on me, once I had lost my mobile in Madurai... You should know about a girl who made me a hero, she saved me from bullying, was the first one in my college to not call me a psycho, and loved this psycho...you should know about a girl who stood and waited for me until my exams were over...you should know about a girl who gave me the initial money to buy the camera. If I could compare myself with a chamber of vacuum, then she is the first drop of air that is coming through the nozzle to fill it. She shaped me as a person, dictated my habits and I'm sure, apart from my mom no one can love me more than she does. She is nothing short of a miracle, no instrument can be used to measure the amount of love she has towards me. She never left me uncared and she knows every single detail of me. Life was something else for me, it went hopeless, and then she came in as hope."

"Joseph, I'm eager to see her"

"You'll see her, and once you do, you cannot resist yourself from starting a debate on which one is beautiful, whether waves from her hair or waves from the ocean? closer to the ocean…you cannot escape from seeing a group of fishes getting jealous of seeing her eyes… You should know the girl, who has the most beautiful eyes in the world, those pair of eyes has a world in it, which is her world, and Alyssa…you should know those eyes that saw me, took me, cared for me, and showered on me the infinite love, you should know that its 'Adina.'"

❋ ❋ ❋

"Indeed, that was a beautiful night," said Alyssa and Adina cried even more but this time the emotions were not the same though. She looked at Joseph.

Joseph who was slightly far from Adina and Alyssa felt bad and said "Ruined it…completely ruined it, thanks to you both for coming here and ruining my love all the way from Australia".

He took his bike in frustration and a chilled palm held his left hand. It was Adina, She gasped and looked at him.

Brandon said, "Yeah that was all right, this is how it should be." Sun slowly started to set in the west.

"Shall we go to Pallam for the sunset?" Adina asked Joseph.

"Are you sure? We were there yesterday right?" he asked.

"Sunsets happen daily, and I want to see every sunset with you," Adina said.

Joseph got emotional and started the bike immediately. Adina asked both Brandon and Alyssa to join them too.

All four headed to Pallam Beach to see the sunset. They went through the streets and had snacks, visited a bangle shop and Alyssa bought half a dozen of the orange color bangles and packed it safely in her bag.

They reached exactly when Sunset. Adina got emotional and she held the arms of Joseph tightly and asked her trademark phrase "Can we be together forever?"

Chapter Four

At Isabella's house, Marthandan and Kaliyan stood with their men on the veranda. The place was so silent that they heard the fallen raindrops drip down the roof and the screeching of the birds somewhere far away. No one uttered a word until the old lady wobbled her way out and asked both of them to kneel. Both looked at each other in anger and kneeled. Mani gave Isabella her favorite snack which is nuts. She ate that sitting on a bench. By that time, Melissa came there in the cycle to give the milk from the church.

On seeing Melissa, both Marthandan and Kaliyan felt embarrassed to kneel in front of her eyes but Isabella didn't allow them to stand up. Melissa parked her cycle and entered the house, poured the milk into a vessel, and left calmly without any sound and she didn't bat an eye at both men.

"I don't think this place is getting any better. Evil has taken over Amboori," said Isabella.

"I think, it is time we move on from both Marthandan and Kaliyan for the search of the next Moothakani," she added looking at their faces closely.

"I still remember how you both used to be in your teens. That is why this entire Amboori believed in you both, but you are just tormenting the minds of people in the village," she said.

Both Marthandan nor Kaliyan didn't look at Isabella, they didn't even lift their head. Stayed knelt.

"Is this why, Lord Krishna got crucified for your sins? My lord is still here, he can watch all your actions. One day he'll show the world, what a lord can do," Isabella slowly blabbered and Mani took her into the house asking both the men to leave the place.

They left along with their men. The rain had just settled down.

The entire Aavani Street gathered outside their houses that morning as Kaliyan walked towards his house. He saw everyone in the street and read disappointment on their faces. He spoke nothing and entered his house, and saw Valli doing her own business and didn't care about him. Suddenly a small girl wearing only a skirt ran in and jumped on Kaliyan's shoulders and kissed him, he smiled lifting her up, and said, "What is Cinderella doing in the skirt? Where is her school uniform?"

The girl smiled and replied, "She is waiting for her guardian angel to take her to her school".

"Ponni, get down and wear your uniform, it's already late," said Valli in a harsh tone.

"Teacher, please don't call me by that name, I know I'm Cinderella, change my name please," said the little girl. "Yes teacher," Kaliyan added.

Valli gave a stern look at Kaliyan and he left the girl and she ran away to wear the uniform. He came near to Valli, who was still folding the dresses of kids, and asked,

"Where did you stay last night?"

"Is that even your concern?" she asked in the same harsh tone.

He looked at her without any words and she looked back at him and said "At the church."

"Was she there?" he quietly asked.

"Where else would she be?" Valli said continuing her work.

"I warned you not to go near Melissa at any cause, I ordered you to stay here," he shouted.

Valli stopped her work and turned at him talking back "Am I born to your father? Or Am I your wife? Who am I to stay here? Give me a good answer, and I'll stay. I'm here for those five orphan kids, I'm a teacher and I owe to educate them. Other than that, I know how to save my ass, Sorry."

She moved away as Ponni also known as Cinderella got ready for school along with the other four kids and all five waved at Kaliyan, who fake smiled at them, not because he disliked them but because he was in a dislikable situation.

✱　✱　✱

Valli walked those five kids through the village and she crossed the center point of Amboori village, which is Sasthan temple. She took a minute and got blessings from the God Sasthan, who was known to be the clan deity of the entire Kanikar. They continued their journey towards the school. There was a tea shop and a small mess which was maintained by Mani, who was in his mid-twenties. He was an assistant to Isabella as well as a traditional supervisor of the village. People would be sitting in that shop and chit-chat about something.

On their way, they also met Father Benjamin known as Ben who was around sixty-five years old almost serving for Amboori church for more than three decades then. He had always worn a gown since the last time the Sasthan pooja and Palli festival happened. He asked them,

"Valli, how are you? Is everything fine? Melisa said that you stayed in church last night. I was out of the station for a month and I was told there were numerous flurries happening over the village. I missed all the fun"

"Yes Father, but everything is fine now. Praise the Lord" replied Valli.

"Praise the Lord…I hope the school is progressing well. If you're in need of help regarding the school and studies, you should contact me. Do not hesitate, and may peace be with you," Father blessed and moved.

Then he stopped and asked, "Valli, how about Sasthan pooja, atleast this year? Who is initiating? What about Kaliyan and Marthandan?"

"Father, that is beyond my knowledge, you should ask them," she said.

"Huh! If only the Sasthan pooja happens, we should also be able to conduct our "Palli" carnival in our church. It has been a long time since…"

He moved and crossed the Sasthan temple and saw the statue of Sasthan along with Vadamala bootham and Vettikadu bootham; the forest deities, the people of Kanikars worship.

Valli then reached the school, a small building with a damaged board, "Kanikar Welfare Board School, Amboori, Thiruvananthapuram district."

There were totally only seventeen students to study in that school which was run by Valli. It was built ten years ago by Moothakani John Kutty, who is no more. He was also the nephew of Isabella. The school was yet to get government approval as there was no Moothakani to take it forward. Valli seemed to be thinking about the conversation she had with Kaliyan, and she put an end to it, before beginning the classes.

✳ ✳ ✳

At Chithirai Street, Marthandan was lying in his house while Mullan massaged his knee as he knelt for some hours before Isabella.

"I shouldn't have looked at her eyes, Mulla," he muttered about Melissa.

"I don't think you looked into her eyes. You just feel embarrassed to have let her see you in that state. Was she present there at Parapan's funeral yesterday?" asked Mullan.

"She was there in every place we went yesterday. Don't know, maybe a coincidence," he mumbled in his sleepy voice. Out of the blue, he heard someone calling out his name loudly from outside the house.

He got up and opened the door screen to see Father Ben standing and shouting his name.

"Praise the Lord Father. What is the issue?" he wondered.

"Issues? Why are there always 'issues' around Marthandan? Is that a wish?" asked Father Ben.

"Nothing I wish Father. It's all about fate," Marthandan said this out of pain, Mullan was pulling a sarcastic look at him without any reaction.

"Marthanda, I know you from your younger days. I thought you were the one to lead the way. You started it for our village but look at you now, with a clumsy beard and dirty t-shirt, and hanging out with a friend like him," Father said to him pointing at Mullan.

"The hardest part of all is, you both didn't get married, that ruins my satisfaction," said Father.

"Father, I got married twice and divorced twice, both live two streets from here and happily married to another man..." said Mullan.

Father stopped him and said, "I didn't talk about you."

Marthandan looked at Father.

"You and Kaliyan, I wished more good things happen to you both," said Father and now Marthandan stopped Father and asked, "Father enough, please...I beg you... please."

"Okay, with all the blessings of almighty, the Sasthan poojaa should happen alongside our Palli's Church festival. Isabella should agree to this, bearing all the odds she puts with respect to her semi-cracked mind. You should talk to her and Melissa," said Father.

Marthandan looked down and stood without uttering a word and Mullan pushed him to agree to the father. But Marthandan stood unmoved.

Father then walked away from the place.

Mullan asked, "Eda, listen to me. It is time to break the shackles. Everything is coming in line. Father supports you…"

"What kind of support? He was asking about him! Is that the kind of support you are talking about?" he yelled back at Mullan.

He stayed silent.

"The place needs a head, the place needs me. It should be made better. You know that school that girl Valli runs? The government has not even approved that. Who cares? And he is asking for me to conduct a festival which is of no use," he yelled out in anxiety.

"Okay okay…, you don't need to engage with her. But please don't make unnecessary talks like this," said Mullan.

He realized his anxiety and looked at himself in the mirror closely for some time. He began to hear several noises in his ears. Slowly a hand, which was pale green with peeled skin, touched him from behind traveling around his shoulders and neck, and grasped his hair tightly. He was watching all this in the mirror and he saw a black snake that came out of his nose and bit his hand. Suddenly he shook his head and realized that it was all hallucination which attacked him momentarily whenever he got emotional or weak.

He washed his face, went to the backyard, and smoked the cigarette.

"Mulla…Mullaaa…Mullaa….." he called thrice but there was no response. So he came into the house to see Mulla eating mangoes, stuffing his mouth, which was why he couldn't reply.

Marthandan saw him keenly and said, "Mulla, no matter what. I'm going to ask both Isabella and Melissa about the festival."

"Hmm…Hmm…" he nodded.

✳ ✳ ✳

In the evening at Isabella's house, a cycle approached along with the dusk. It was Melissa who bought milk and honey. She parked her cycle at her house. Mani came out of Isabella's house and greeted her with a smile and said,

"Melissa, you bought the milk? Please don't. I already gave her the pure cow milk just now and what are those? Honey? I guess it is not suitable for her health right now. Get in, talk to her and you'll feel the truth. Take care of her."

Mani left for his place. The dusk completely covered the light but Melissa was still sitting outside in the heavy wind.

She felt disappointed that Mani had given the milk already to Isabella. They both were responsible for taking care of Isabella. So she decided to give her something before she saw her. She went to her backyard and found nothing. Then, she came back and sat at her door again.

As she was inhaling the heavy breeze of Amboori, she listened to Isabella's voice from inside the house.

"May the almighty save us, save our village, the son of God, our messiah, in the name of the holy spirit, bless us."

She went in to see Isabella kneeling and praying in front of Lord Krishna's statue. She helped her to get up, adjusted her dress, kept the Lord Krishna statue aside, made her sit normally, and asked her,

"What are you doing?"

"Just praying…who told you to come in?" Isabella asked in a calm tone,

She didn't say anything, made the bed with two pillows, and helped Isabella sit comfortably.

"Mani had said something about your health, what was that?" she asked.

Isabella closely looked at her and asked, "Where is your bindi? Women without bindis are equal to those being topless, and you are topless."

"Thanks," she said and she went to the kitchen and made hot water to massage Isabella's legs.

She continued her blabbering then held her hands and said "Dear, your eyes are so powerful. Those two priceless fishes that sail over the ocean of your forehead are prone to hunting, so beware of the hunters. You should protect them with the shield that is the bindi."

Melissa's "bindiless" face lightened up by the definition given by Isabella and continued her work.

"In all my forty years, I haven't seen any hunter born in this village, to catch these fishes. Even if someone does, these fishes can hunt back immediately," she said.

Isabella looked clueless and Melissa continued to knead Isabella's foot with hot water.

"Women without bindi are Goddesses. Bindi kills the beauty of eyes, it breaks the mood of ecstasy for watching eyes to feel the warmth. And yeah women's eyes are powerful but it is after all a pair of eyes with desire, love, lust, wish, disappointment, betrayal, longing yet powerful."

As Melissa said, Isabella fell asleep. Melissa then cleaned her hands and checked her phone to see the time which was five past ten at night. She phoned Valli.

"Where are you?".

"I'm on my way to the Church," said Valli over the phone.

"I'm not in Church, I'm staying tonight here in Isabella's. Please come here," she said.

"Oh, I'm right near the church. I think Father is back here. Let me tell him and come," said Valli walking with her bag towards the Church.

"Okay. I'll wait for you," said Melissa and cut the call.

In the Church, Father Ben was seen sitting alone in a chair and reading the bible. Valli greeted him and kneeled in front of a small Jesus statue.

"Praise the Lord Valli. What brings you here at this time?" asked Father.

"Father, I was staying here for over a month since you were on a pilgrimage tour, I actually denied but Melissa wanted me to stay with her. Sorry father," she said in a hesitant tone.

He smiled and said "Why are you so scared of telling me this, Am I going to charge you a rent? This is not my place, this place belongs to the Holy son of God. Not only this place but our entire world is his house. He is our shepherd…'"

"But, this little sheep doesn't get a place to reside in his house. Maybe I'm an unwanted sheep in his herd," she said with hopeless eyes.

"Valli, you're not alone. We all know who you are and how special you are to this village," Father tried to console her and Valli said "Okay Father, it is already late and Melissa is waiting for me at Isabella's. I have to go,"

Father stopped her and asked her, "Did you talk with Kaliyan about the Sasthan Festival?"

"No Father," as Valli said this, a dim light entered the door of the church. Kaliyan stopped his bike and entered the church.

She ignored his arrival and started to walk away. He entered while she left the church. He looked at her without a word and asked the Father,

"Where is she going now?"

"Melissa called" Father replied. He turned back and looked at her walking faster.

"Kaliyan, I have told you many times before my pilgrimage. Now I'm back here still nothing has changed. When will one of you take over as Moothakani and when does the village go back to being normal?" asked Father.

He replied nothing and looked at Father with a calm face. Father again asked the same thing. Kaliyan replied, "Father, it is my responsibility to make Sasthan pooja and Palli festival happen. I will talk to Isabella and make it happen before him. Praise the Lord."

After saying this, Kaliyan immediately left and started his bike, following Valli. After reaching her, he asked her to get on the bike but she refused and continued walking. He followed her from some distance on the bike. After walking for some distance Valli felt annoyed and got on his bike and said,

"Please, I beg you. At least work on the festival and talk to Isabella about it. This should happen...."

Kaliyan listened to this, started his bike and headed to Isabella's.

At Isabella's, Melissa was sitting outside waiting for Valli and felt relieved after seeing her. Melissa didn't look at Kaliyan's face and neither did Kaliyan. Valli got down and eventually, Kaliyan took his bike and left right away.

"Why are you here?" asked Valli to Melissa.

"Mani is going to Thiruvananthapuram for passport verification. He can't stay the night. So it is my day to take care of Isabella, and also Father has come. He will be taking that room we stayed in last night," Melissa said opening the door to the room. She had made the bed for both. They laid down tiredly.

"Melissa, will you ask me in return if I ask you about your day?" asked Valli.

"If you want to, I'll," said Melissa.

"I don't want to be asked, but everything needs to be told," Valli whispered within her.

Both slowly closed their eyes and the night went calmly dumping all the stories of the people of Amboori.

Chapter Five

Sun slowly rose in Kanyakumari. DySP Arockiyaraj was seen jogging on the streets of Kanyakumari and he reached the western shores of Cape Beach after waving at the sun at its rise. He was jogging alone without any other policemen and force or jeep. He was having pure buttermilk and had some fiber biscuits on his jogging. He then stopped at a platform, tied his shoelace, and sat for a few minutes. Meanwhile, he was approached by two men, wearing a white t-shirt but without jogging shoes, who came and sat beside him, with him in the middle.

"Morning, sir," said the man who sat to the right of Arockiyaraj.

Arockiyaraj didn't give a greeting eye at them but just nodded his head a bit.

The man who was sitting at the left took his mobile and called someone and said,

"Anna we are here, you can come and make the conversation."

Arockiyaraj observed them and felt something fishy over there and started thinking, after a while he said.

"Brothers, let me come instead and have a deeper conversation with whoever you were talking with." He decided to go and crack this fishy thing immediately rather than having this around here in this pleasant early morning at the cape of India,

Both the men saw each other and took him immediately in their car and drove it to a fishing yard nearby.

Arockiyaraj got down and saw the place, he also saw a fish vendor having his freshly taken fish from the sea to his containers, and suddenly he was tapped on the shoulders from the back. He turned to see Peter Durai standing with his men,

"Good morning sir, how is our land? Hope you are enjoying" Peter asked.

"Yeah…so far so nice," Arockiyaraj said and smiled at him.

The sea breeze along with the smell of the fish yard united well enough to create the heat of the situation there. There was the big guy, Peter Durai started explaining about him to Arockiyaraj.

"Sir, it is already a late morning for you people. You have to get to the office right? Let me get straight to the point, this is Peter Durai, in fact, Peter Durai…, huh, okay enough. You already must have heard my caste surname because I'm better known by the people in that way. I may look young and I'm still single but the thing is I need to settle down all these flurries and hurries as soon as before I reach my thirty. I had my uncle who is a distant relative of mine here as DySP before. Unfortunately, he got transferred…and that is because of me as well caught up with a pride killing case near Aralvaimozhi."

Arockiyaraj looked straight at him and suddenly looked at the fish vendor and asked about the rate of the fish.

Peter Durai looked at his men and again continued his speech,

"Sir, that doesn't sound funny I guess. Things may get ever colder now, listen to me…I belong to a higher caste within the state and I'm younger among the political leaders here in my place and I don't want to waste my time doing these things for my respectable place in my caste. All I need is money. For that, I need to give tons of money exceeding my fellow caste men to go to that place in any political party and I want my caste to reign over the state and rule the people as they did before. So, I continued doing my weed supplies which began ten years ago. The boy said you are not from our community and you won't be adhering to us but sir, you are from Ramnad district and you definitely must have known what we guys are doing here…I can still provide you with whatever you want. Just withdraw the case and enjoy the scenic beauty of Cape Comorin…"

"How much a KG?" Arockiyaraj asked to Fish vendor.

Peter Durai raged on after Arockiyaraj who was not giving any attention to any of the words he just spoke.

"Arockiyaraj, even my patience has its levels," he warned him.

He bought the fish and asked him to pay for the fish as he didn't bring enough money rather the fish vendor didn't have Gpay fascility either. Peter's face changed and he paid three hundred and fifty rupees to the vendor. He was a bit relieved as he asked him to pay which felt like the acceptance of his deal and he said,

"Thank you, sir. You will be treated well here and you are clever. Other people won't be living peacefully without our mercy here."

"Man, I can arrest and take charge against you right here, right now, but you will be free immediately…I want you to be caught red-handed and I will see your face and will return this debt of three hundred and fifty rupees when you are under arrest with my handcuff tightening your wrists…I bet now on my debt that this fish is your party for your jail life. Bye, it's already eight o clock have to go and roast the fish,"

Peter looked shocked in anger and Arockiyaraj hired an auto and left the place.

❋ ❋ ❋

Meanwhile, at the same eight o'clock, Abraham woke up from his sleep and checked his mobile. He was called by his mom at once.

"What are you doing with your mobile early in the morning even before you are completely awakened," his mother shouted from the kitchen.

Soon, Abraham rushed out of his bed, ran to the kitchen, and asked, "How did you know?"

"So, you were using a mobile?" asked his mother and laughed, "I just did it to wake you up," she added. Abraham pushed the utensils from the shelves that were placed to rest on one other. They all fell which made a heavy noise in the house.

Adina rushed from the bathroom with wet hair and dress and checked on his mother. Simultaneously, her father Christopher Raj also rushed from the hall to check on his wife.

In the kitchen, Adina was standing in a wet dress and wet hair. On looking at this her father shouted at her and asked her to get inside and looked at Abraham who stared back at his father before leaving that place.

Adina went to her bedroom, sat, and started to cry because of her father's arrogant act. Then her mother came in and wiped her hair and started giving her usual consolation.

"What did I do? Why does he hate me?" asked Adina in a crying tone to her mother.

"It is not your fault, either his. It is all about how these things are made," said her mother tapping her head.

"Not his? Mom, please prove to me that I was born to him. He never talked to me with kindness, he never wished me for my birthdays, and in fact, he never phoned me at least once, and Mom? You support him right? Typical Indian woman…" said Adina furiously yet in a crying tone.

"It is already late, chin up and have your breakfast, I'll pack your lunch…" her mom didn't care about her words and said casually.

Adina again cried saying, "Never, I never take anything from this cruel house." Her mom looked at her simultaneously looking at the Jesus painting in her room and walked away.

Abraham got ready for college and took his bike. His mom stopped him, put Adina's lunch box in his bag, asked him to drop Adina at the bus stand, and said,

"Don't forget to give this to her",

She was running late with all the short ruckus that happened just before.

After having a quick breakfast with swollen eyes, she packed her bag and got ready for the office. She saw her brother waiting for her on the bike with a disgusted face as he was forced to do this job.

She crossed her dad, who was sitting outside in a chair reading a newspaper. She moved from there without a word and stopped for a second to send a text to Joseph,

"Do not come to the bus stand, I'm with my brother," she sent through SMS and got on the bike. On their ride to the bus stand, she was inching to start a conversation with her brother but she was a bit hesitant as he never cared about her.

But after some time, she saw their favorite ice cream parlor where their father used to take them to eat ice cream when they were kids. She decided to cut off her ego and asked her brother to stop at that ice cream parlor. He eventually stopped there and turned back to her and said,

"This is why you're the worst nuisance ever. Do you know how old I am? Please don't drag me into your emotional circles, please stay away from me. Today is the last time I take you in my bike, which is too for the sake of my mother who asked for it,"

As she was listening to everything from the rear seat, her face froze but her eyes worked quickly to shed tears which was designated for this scenario. He quickly started his bike and moved. The blowing wind cleanly wiped the tears from Adina's eyes.

✱ ✱ ✱

A few miles away, Joseph was watching TV, holding the remote on one hand and the food on the other. His mom, who was working as a teacher was getting ready for the school. She didn't interrupt Joseph as he was keenly watching the Discovery Channel 'Food Factory' show, where they were showing how potato chips were made in the industry.

"I think this show should be telecasted regularly," said his mom. Joseph looked at her with a doubtful face,

Mom replied, "I guess, only during this show your mobile getting some rest".

He didn't care about that and soon realized it was time, and he should have checked his phone for Adina's text.

He rushed to see his phone lying in his bed without charge and it was switched off. He patted his head, plugged the phone into the charger, and rushed to get ready asking his mom to keep the key behind the floor mat. He started his bike and stopped suddenly. He realized that he hadn't taken his phone and he rushed back to his room and unplugged the charger and moved. He suddenly stopped again because the switch was not on. He gasped and smiled with pain, put the phone in his pocket, ran to his bike, and started it again.

His mom was watching all these and immediately changed the channel to watch her favorite stuff.

Joseph was driving his bike in superfast mode from his house to the bus stand to arrive at the time when Adina would.

Abraham drove his bike and reached the bus stand, as soon as Adina got down he turned his bike and rushed back to his institution for the crash course.

Adina took her handkey, placed it on her eyes, and closed it. Then she opened it to see Joseph standing with his bike. She immediately got tensed and hissed,

"I told you not to come today. Abraham was here..."

"What was he doing here?" asked Joseph.

Adina was about to say something, but suddenly she heard her brother's bike and turned back only to see Abraham, who was standing and throttling his bike along with the lunch box he forgot to give.

Adina's hand was shivering in fear when she received that lunch box. Meanwhile Abraham and Joseph looked at each other and they both didn't speak a word.

"My father is right, you're not the one he expected, you bitch," he scolded her right in the middle of the road.

"That is not right brother," Joseph interfered in their conversation and Abraham stopped him and pushed him away. By then Joseph sensed some smell from Abraham which was familiar to him in the recent past.

"Listen, please don't tell this to dad. He already hates me, I beg you," she pleaded.

"Don't be worried. It is time you evicted from our place, you bloody bitch, and I'm ashamed that you are part of my family," he scolded her back. She started crying and the crowd intervened with them and Abraham swiftly started his bike and went away from that place. Joseph made her hop on the bike and took her away from that place.

On their way, he called Brandon and asked both Brandon and Alyssa to come to his studio at Ransom town.

* * *

At their Guest house, Alyssa and Brandon were connected through Zoom with their Australian mates for a conversation. They were happily talking and Brandon who attended Joseph's phone call understood the situation and signaled Alyssa to get ready to go there.

"I think we have to solve another curious case of Adina and Joseph" he said and she smiled and reacted in a funny way and continued to chat through video call.

She was asked about the fun she was having in India. Suddenly one of the guys in the group call asked,

"Hey Alyssa, what did you buy for her?"

Alyssa's face turned to pale for a second and she immediately resumed talking,

"Yeah, I bought her very much of a traditional Indian type of bangles, which we will never see in Australia..." By telling this her eyes started to shed drops of tears unknowingly as she bought this in a very emotional mental space. Every drop of her tear had a million volume of love in it.

Shortly before hanging up the call, Alyssa greeted them in the call to talk later, and she finally asked before cutting the call,

"Take care of Erica...Tell her I miss her and I'm sure, she will be off the bed soon."

She closed the laptop and they both reached Joseph's studio.

When the door was opened to them with the knock, they both entered to see Adina sitting with her hands placed on her head.

"Is everything okay?" asked Alyssa.

"No, her father might get to know about our love now," replied Joseph.

"Ohh, that's great mate. It's a great time to take your love to the next level, don't you think?" asked Brandon excitedly.

She started crying slightly and Brandon noticed her and said,

"Oh no, I think Adina isn't ready for this, Joseph. I think you should wait until she feels ready to get married." Adina cried harder and started crying loudly.

"Why is she increasing the frequency of her crying with every passing second?" asked Brandon.

"You don't get it. It will create so many problems and we might end up losing each other," he was worried and it was evident in those words he uttered.

Brandon and Alyssa looked at each other and he asked "Do you understand anything?, I don't…".

Alyssa nodded her head.

Suddenly Adina's phone rang but she didn't pick it. She refused to because she was so much caught up with crying which didn't let her focus on anything external.

"Okay, what do you expect me to do? We have two days here before our VISA expires. We have to find the medicine and…" As Brandon was saying this Adina's phone rang again.

He stopped talking and he felt disturbed and asked her to attend the phone.

Adina, in the middle of crying, took out the phone from her bag. She instantly stopped crying as soon as she saw the phone screen. The phone rang continuously. Joseph saw this and he went to see the phone screen getting hit by the same wave of shock.

Brandon then decided to go and asked Alyssa to follow him and he stood shocked as well and so did Alyssa on seeing the phone screen as it read, "Dad."

Adina grabbed guts from her god and attended the call and said, "Praise the Lord"

Chapter Six

"You're not the only one, these sufferings belong to every woman in the world. Who are they to restrict you? Who are they to abuse you? Who are they to decide your moves? Wake up and rise above patriarchy, now open your eyes to see the cliff of the world…"

Mellissa opened her eyes to see herself standing on the cliff of the Dravyapara at the Mountain and the panic of death was seen in her eyes. She was constantly hearing the voice that kept saying,

"Go beyond, go beyond…go beyond"

Melissa shook her head to deny what the voice said behind her. Then the voice said,

"Okay, turn around and see me…turn around and see me, look at my image, and decide about being a woman here…"

She panicked again and she suddenly turned back to see a nude young woman standing in a flash. Instantly, she slipped and fell from the hilltop.

She suddenly woke up from the sleep letting out a minute scream before she realized that it was all just a dream. But it felt more like a nightmare. It was early in the morning and the sun was slowly rising in the east.

Valli woke up along with her and asked "What was it?" while she tied her hair up.

"Was it you?" asked Melissa to Valli.

"What?" she wondered.

"That nude woman" she slowly said.

"What? When was I nude? Did you see me nude?" She got anxious, adjusted her saari, and rushed up from the bed. Melissa asked her to relax and calm down. Then she went to wash her face and looked for Isabella.

She was seen in her room, knelt before the statues of Lord Krishna and Jesus Christ, closely looking at them, under a thin yellow candlelight that almost covered the entire house. Melissa with a sleepy voice asked Isabella,

"Shall I get you some water?"

She didn't respond.

"Shall I get you some milk and honey?" she asked again.

She didn't respond again. Melissa then took those statues away, and immediately Isabella reacted and said,

"Why are you taking my stuff away?" Melissa calmly replied, "Please tell me who they are and I'll keep them aside."

She hesitated and said slowly, "My messiah."

"Who?" she asked

"The one who saved people," the old lady slowly answered.

"Who is the one?" she asked again.

The yellow light from the candle slowly faded from the house with the entry of the same yellow-colored sunrays from the east.

Isabella started thinking and when she was about to answer, they heard someone knocking on the door. Melissa kept the statue then and there and went to open the door.

She stood in shock when she opened the door.

It was Marthandan who came to speak with Isabella and Melissa as per Father Ben's words. He saw the bright face of her from the very light yellowish sunlight, and he saw her lips crumbling between them. Her eyeballs started to widen in surprise as she hadn't seen Marthandan this close for so many years. Her hair tried to hide her cheeks that shivered but her forehead stood straight against him.

He didn't utter a word as he was mesmerized by the early morning yellowish face and her orange lips which were tightly closed to restrict from speaking any word. The rose petals on their plants outside the house decided to bloom and the sunflowers around the house turned east to welcome their beloved.

Mullan who sat down in half-sleep with a scarf around his head and mouth slowly said,

"Staring competition, it seems."

Slowly the clouds moved away to help the sun to spread more shine towards Amboori. Marthandan called "Mani.... Mani...."

Valli slowly came out from the house and said, "Mani went to Thiruvananthapuram, only Isabella and us are here, what is the issue?"

"Oh, Eda Marthanda…you're so familiar with "issues" here?". He punched him lightly and replied to Valli,

"I want to talk to Isabella amma about the festival."

"What festival?" she asked and gave a look at Melissa who moved away and started grabbing flowers from the plants.

"Sasthan pooja and Palli festival…" he replied. Melissa listened to everything from the garden.

To their surprise, a bike sound slowly arose in that early morning. It was Kaliyan who came alone to Isabella's house. He parked the bike, opened the gate, and entered the house with his sunglasses. Valli immediately came to Kaliyan and asked furiously,

"Are you here to mess up the situation again?"

"I'm not in the mood to talk with you, please make way," he said subtly.

Mullan, who was still half asleep, commented, "Eda Marthanda, have you heard about a man who holds an umbrella at midnight?" He nodded.

"Do you know what he is doing now?" he continued, and he nodded again.

"He is now wearing sunglasses even before the sun arrives. What a brilliant move saare…" he commented and laughed. Marthandan joined the laughter session with a kinky sarcastic smile and looked at Kaliyan, who was standing alone with sunglasses still on.

"Mani…Mani…Mani…" Kaliyan shouted.

"Wow, I never knew sound waves travel to Thiruvananthapuram from here. Nice volume. It would have passed Aryan code now, sooner it will reach the capital, Kollaa, " Mullan again commented on Kaliyan sarcastically and laughed.

"Is this what you wanted in the early morning?" Valli asked.

Meanwhile, Melissa completed a revolution of the house, plucked all kinds of flowers, and came back to the veranda. Sun has taken charge for the day.

She kept all the flowers near the door and made it into a bouquet-like. Isabella came out slowly, and Mullan immediately splashed away his curtain getting refreshed, and stood up. Isabella slowly came near and took the flower bouquet, looked up, and said, "Hail the lord Krishna". Everyone greeted Isabella as the day had just started, she sat near the door and sang a song praising Jesus Christ.

That old Malayalam song, "Ambadi poonkuyile" she used to sing every morning, and everyone listened to that song patiently for her to start the day.

As everyone stood silent, Isabella grabbed the flowers that Melissa had, and held them on her head. She then started walking from the house. All the others followed her way as well. Kaliyan locked his bike and kept up with them.

As they passed, Isabella started singing the song she just listened. On their way the people of Amboori greeted Isabella equally as their deity and all the others; Melissa, Valli, Kaliyan, Marthandan, and Mullan followed her.

After reaching Sasthan temple, she stopped singing and took the flowers from her basket, threw some flowers, looked at the sky, and said,

"She is still angry, she is still looking at us, those eyes! Those eyes are terrifying…she won't spare us…" in a shaky voice.

Everyone joined her, got amazed by her sayings, and looked at each other, Immediately Melissa held her and asked her to calm down and Valli joined her and asked,

"Whom does she talk about?"

Melissa's eyes lit up and she shook her head implementing that she had no idea. Valli got more curious and asked the same again. Marthandan asked Mullan to call Father Benjamin and inform this.

Kaliyan who was watching everything, came to her, grabbed her hand, and asked her to leave. A few minutes later Father Ben arrived at the temple. He received blessings from her feet and took her in his bike with the help of Melissa at the back. Melissa took the flower basket from Isabella and made sure she was safe and comfortable on the bike. Marthandan and Mullan were watching this. Kaliyan started his bike and asked Valli to sit. She hesitated and refused to sit on the bike. He slapped her hard which made both Marthandan and Mullan turn at them.

Mullan got furious and stepped towards Kaliyan but Marthandan immediately stopped him. Kaliyan glared at Mullan with a determined cunning face, and Marthandan also looked at Kaliyan.

Meanwhile, Father started his bike and Melissa held Isabella for safety. Marthandan looked at Melissa and she turned her head to check at him but turned back in a fraction of a second after noticing that he was looking at her. All his young days' charms were brought back into his mind.

When their eyes met, his heart and mind combined to conduct a catastrophe and all the clouds appeared before him. The entire Western Ghats breeze of Amboori slayed him, the power of Melissa's eyes even in her forties took him a minute to recover from.

It was so long ago that it happened, he never really knew when it happened in recent days, because Melissa consistently and carefully avoided his sight at all costs. So when it finally happened, he lost his presence and started being on cloud nine.

At the church, Isabella was taken inside with the help of Melissa. Then Father approached the stage and lighted the candle. She bought the basket of flowers and gave them to Isabella.

The old lady just looked at the statue of the crucified Jesus.

She looked at Jesus's eyes closely and saw the blood painting that was drawn on his face as if it was flowing down from the thorn crown on his head. She immediately started murmuring something which Melissa noted and she felt like something was wrong with the old lady.

"The same thorn she wore…" she whispered.

Melissa came closer and asked her to remain silent as the entire church was now like an arena of silence. The smell of half-melted wax and the oil residues gave the breeze that no one could feel, except Melissa who was always fond of these fragrances right from her teens.

Isabella continued her whisperings and again looked at the statue closely and saw the blood paintings slowly dropping down. The dhoti on the statue swayed with the wind.

She continued to give a close look at the statue and suddenly closed her eyes and heard something in her mind.

"I'm not who I am. I am supposed to be someone you never imagined," some incorporeal voice said this in a gloomy vision and it repeated twice. Suddenly, she was shaken by Melissa who gave the flower from the basket, which was now tied. Isabella asked Melissa to lift her to reach the desired height for garlanding.

Meanwhile, Father Ben came inside along with the VAO of Amboori, Mr. Ayyapan Kutty to grant permission for the Sasthan festival to happen along with the Palli Festival for this church. Ayyapan saw Isabella garlanding Jesus and was shocked to see a woman of this age trying hard for this. Ayyapan, who was a newly appointed VAO of this village asked about the old lady with Father Ben.

"She is one hundred and seventeen years old and she is half Christian and half Hindu. Her worship is wild. Never knew how this had become her habit some say some stories. But what I heard is about some trauma she had back in 1940s."

Father Ben vividly explains about Isabella to VAO, who was curiously listening to it.

"What happened in 1940?" asked VAO.

"I think it was the loss of her husband. She was born as a Kanikar without Hinduism and Christianity. But it all changed when she saw her husband who was a Christian inside our tribe. They got converted by our missionaries some years ago. Things were different back then, right? In the holy name of Jesus Christ, people used to say, that converting lower-status people into our religion is quite easier but here in this part of the world, the tribes are considered as low status among the others. But not by themselves. They are the king of this southwestern ghats. They claim that this is their thing. So, it bears that the Christians at that time gained the help of Hindu Gods to convert people," Father calmly explained while VAO interrupted,

"But how?"

"Missionaries at that time closely claimed that Jesus and Krishna are the same. Jesus was original and the Hindu versions were just fabricated ones and asked them to completely convert to "The Original Christianity". That is where this confusion and mental trance of Isabella would have begun probably along with her husband's loss. But only she can answer with the truth." As Father Ben said this and walked by, he hit Melissa who was on his way out from the church.

She was stopped and introduced to VAO by Father. But Melissa gave a very tiny smile, which was as tiny as a grain of sand, and walked outside towards the pathway.

She got frustrated and suddenly she was sweating heavily as she was not comfortable with seeing new men. She looked up to the sky and saw the clouds covering the sun with the gloomy climate. She took her saree end to wipe the sweat, and looked down to see Marthandan standing with the rose flowers with thorns he plucked inside the church.

Her anxiety increased. The gloomy windless climate added an extra spice to her suffocation. He who didn't know any of her inner calamities, took a rose from his hands and stretched his arms towards her.

She now heard nothing in the world but the famous engine sound of Kaliyan's motorbike approaching. He stopped his bike and came into the church. Seeing Marthandan holding a rose, he came near him.

Isabella, who was just praying inside the church looking at the statue of the crucified Jesus, suddenly started chanting for Krishna.

"Hare Krishna Hare Krishna…Krishna Krishna Hare hare…" she repeated thrice and both Father Ben and VAO looked at her weird chants inside the church.

Simultaneously, Kaliyan tapped the shoulders of Marthandan and waved at him to talk,

For Melissa, this sudden tap on the shoulders of Marthandan by Kaliyan felt like a thunder hit her head. She couldn't see that thing happening again in front of her after a long time. He turned at him and looked at his face.

Her eyes rolled up along with the "Hare Krishna…" chants by Isabella and she rapidly collapsed and fainted on the floor.

Father Ben and VAO rushed up to her and took her in.

Marthandan was stunned at the same place, still holding the flowers he bought for her. Kaliyan had no clue what just happened in front of him.

He saw Melissa being taken into the church by Father Ben and VAO and all he could do was just stand and watch this thing as the sunlight fell straight across his face. After a few seconds of doing nothing, Kaliyan now again tapped the shoulders of Marthandan. He showed signs of anger and he suddenly held his flowers and slapped Kaliyan's face in his own way.

He fell immediately and his face started to bleed with the thorns of the roses he had in his hands. Just before he realized that he was bleeding, he was hit by another slap. After resisting for some time, Kaliyan used his legs to make him fall down, grabbed his head, and hit it on the ground.

He groaned in pain and Kaliyan stood up on his knees and punched his face thrice. Marthandan endeavored to hold Kaliyan's hands and bit his wrist, making him lose his strength. He again took the roses and slapped his face and neck, but Kaliyan on the floor kicked the balls of Marthandan and made him fall again. Slowly Kaliyan stood up, picked up those roses, and slapped at Marthandan's face. Marthandan's cheeks also started to bleed.

Father Ben saw them from inside and shouted not to fight. Isabella stood up and came near to the bible table and saw something being written in bolder ink on the top of The Bible.

Both Father and VAO rushed to the pathway to stop them from fighting.

"This is satanic, you morons you are not supposed to fight inside the Church's premises. This is the holy place of love. Pull yourselves together and get over it already," shouted Father Ben. VAO held Marthandan from the back who was lying down on the ground.

Kaliyan who was so furious, screamed like hell and took a bunch of roses and tried to slap Marthandan but missed the target and ended up puncturing VAO's cheek.

"Jesus Christ…Mr. Ayyapan Kutty!" Father shouted and tried to stop Kaliyan and held him back.

Now VAO screamed like hell and got furious with one another and grabbed the leftover roses and tried to slap Kaliyan. But again the same story happened. Kaliyan evaded the slap and the thorns of beautiful roses ended up getting imprinted on Father Ben's face.

Inside the church, Isabella finally tried hard to read the bold-lettered verse of bible from Mathew 5:39,

"But I say to you, if someone slaps you on the right cheek, offer the other cheek also".

Complete silence prevailed for a few seconds and the wind blew some roses that swayed across the pathway. The entire rose petals turned into blood.

Chapter Seven

Joseph rode his bike in a haste and Brandon and Alyssa followed him. Adina who was sitting behind him was crying her eyes out. Meanwhile, in the rush, he turned back and consoled her on the way. Traffic signals played a role in adding more suffering to this situation. The phone call she received from her father was the root cause of that situation. They rushed to Hospital Road from Ransom Town and reached Government Hospital, Kanyakumari. He dropped her at the gate and asked Alyssa to join her. Both women hurried into the reception of the casualty ward and she saw her father sitting on a chair with his head down towards the floor. She slowly went near him. By seeing her feet, Christopher Raj recognized it was Adina and he lifted his head up. She was already in tears and she was unable to control it when she saw her father's red eyes.

He didn't speak a word but continued staring at his daughter. Her mother came to the place with medicines in her hand and cried on seeing her daughter. Alyssa watching all this, just stood still as she wasn't able to emote properly.

"Where is he?" asked Adina.

Her mother pointed her fingers towards the direction of the ICU.

She immediately closed her mouth with her palms and cried even harder. Alyssa texted Joseph, "Abraham is in ICU."

He was at the gate and he showed the text he received to Brandon,

"Should we go in? Or we should stay up here all night?"

"Let's do the right thing…" he said, which made Brandon go blank.

Adina and her mom entered near the ICU but the staff didn't allow them. They were waiting for a few minutes, and suddenly she saw a doctor getting into her brother's ICU ward. She stopped him and asked about his condition.

He had a glance at the reports and said, "Nothing to worry about. Just an overdose of Marijuana that made him fall off from bike. No serious injuries, we'll clear it up."

She slowly looked at her father who was still in the same state except his heart. It shattered down. He slowly looked up at her with tears brimming over his eyes. She rushed to her father, held his hands, and asked him not to worry about Abraham.

"This is not how I brought him up. This is not the way he should have turned up. How will I face the people of our clan? How will I have a mic at church? Where did those speeches go?" he worried deeply about his son and as long as she could remember, it was the first time her father had spoken in sentences with her. Adina knelt in front of her father silently without a word but tears fell down her cheeks.

"You don't have anything to say?" he asked.

Adina slowly said, "I forgot the word I used to call you".

His face was shattered with her words and he closed his eyes.

Alyssa texted Joseph, "Everything is fine".

Joseph and Brandon got relieved and called Alyssa out.

She went to Adina and signaled her that she was leaving. Adina nodded her head and Alyssa held her hands in a sign of hope and said "Take care, we'll be here." She also acknowledged her mom and started to leave the place.

While she crossed the oncology outpatient department, she stood for a second and had a glance at that place, which was dirty and unclean. She saw the patients lying on untidy beds and benches. She could see the unhygienic biowastes and cotton with blood strains. She also could see some people who were drained out and seemed to fall off the benches. She went inside with a mask on and took photos of that place.

When she turned to return, she was stopped by a very small girl child about the age of five. That child grabbed the skirt of Alyssa and asked her to come down. She went down on her knees and smiled at her, and the kid smiled back.

"What's your name?" she asked.

The little kid couldn't understand what she'd been asked and caressed her soft and silky hair. She understood that the kid couldn't understand. She started using actions.

She pointed towards herself and said, "I'm Alyssa, A-L-Y-S-S-A, now tell me yours."

The kid smiled slowly and said, "Parvathy…"

"Nice name, why are you here? Who brought you?" she asked with a happy smile.

Suddenly the ward assistant shouted, "Parvathy…"

Parvathy waved a bye with that same smile and ran back to the ward assistant.

Alyssa followed the kid Parvathy, she saw Parvathy being taken on a chair. She looked at that from there and she saw her head being tonsured by someone there. All that Alyssa could hear was Parvathy's resistant screaming. The entire place looked horrifying to her and her ears only could earn the scream from that little child. All the people lying on beds and benches seemed to stare at her and the sound of heavy frequency dumped her ears, which made her close her eyes only to see Parvathy smiling creepily with a shaven head. She immediately opened her eyes and left the place with a heavy heart and came out of the ward. She looked back at the "Oncology department" board and took a picture of it.

Meanwhile, Adina's mother nudged her and asked, "Who is that foreigner?" Adina hesitated first and started saying, "Ma, she is…" and she was immediately interrupted by a harsh voice from three policemen raised at her father. He pleaded not to file a case or complaint against his son.

"Sir he is innocent, he's my son and he is a student," he pleaded.

"Students are not meant to have cannabis in their pockets," said a cop who was strongly built with a steady and fine mustache.

One of the constables said, "He is the newly appointed DySP."

Christopher Raj saw the name badge, "Arockiyaraj Fernandes" in his chest and asked him,

"Sir, I hope you know about our religion, please spare us from this, sir may I know which church you are from? I'll speak with the bishop and let us do you a favor, anything… sir please consider."

"Hello, whom do you think you're? Trying to bribe me uh? By the way, we don't belong to any church, we have our own "Jesus temple and Mary Matha temple" and we don't allow any other community people into our street and our temple, I saw your address. You are from Anjugramam, right? I know which people live over there, you bloody…" Arockiyaraj fumed at him.

Both Adina and her mother were in shock and they were scared about their son's life. Arockiyaraj asked,

"Do you know about him?"

Evangeline started crying and Adina started consoling her.

Arockiyaraj shouted at her to stop crying and said,

"Your son has been smoking weed for over six months which means eventually he would have had a source to buy here. I need that from your son and for that he has to be taken under custody."

All three Adina, her mother, and her father looked at each other and stood in shock.

"Sir, we hope you understand about our family, we are a middle-class self-obsessed religious family. All we know is our almighty Jesus Christ, we never cared for anything apart from him, and all we had was him, but now he is hanging somewhere left us hanging here." Christopher pleaded with the cop Arockiyaraj.

Adina took her mobile and texted all these problems to Joseph.

Joseph received this text outside a tea shop after refreshing Alyssa who was still traumatized by a place she came across a few minutes ago. Brandon was smoking and sprinkling some water on Alyssa's face, completely unaware of what was happening inside. In that tea shop, they played a Hindi song "Kisi Disco Mein Jayee" and he seemed to like that song especially the sound effects of the song so he asked the tea master to increase the volume of the song. In between Joseph wiped Alyssa's face while Brandon seemed to be vibing to that banger. Joseph saw the text he received from Adina and he immediately called her.

Adina went to the restroom to attend the call of Joseph,

Joseph listened to everything amidst "Kisi Disco Mein Jayee" and reacted quickly with Brandon and Alyssa. He explained everything Adina told him.

Suddenly Brandon reacted, "Cannabis?" I think he's my kind of guy.

"Stop joking, this is all about Adina and her family's reputation. We need to find the donor of the cannabis," said Joseph.

"Umm, well how do they decide about a reputation with a pack of cannabis?" asked Brandon,

"Here people do, but Bruh, I can't explain to you right now, tell me about the donors you bought from," Joseph pushed him in a hurry.

"Wait wait, this is scary and unsafe to tell you. See I'm a foreigner and you are getting me in trouble. They might find me and put me in jail, I'm scared man." He lashed out anxiously and also shook his leg for "'Kisi Disco Mein Jayee."

"Listen, Joseph, you are brave you know that and I'm half brave and you also know that but these weed sellers and cops are not even close to brave. We don't want to have any grudge against them. We didn't go to that place, we asked someone in a bar to buy the stuff. It is impossible for people like us to go there, it is a confidential area, I guess it is near some beach," he added and continued vibing for the song.

Joseph saw the text of Adina again and felt anguished again looked at Brandon. Suddenly Alyssa came after refreshing herself with water and asked Joseph.

"I reckon I would have a green now! It's high time that I smoke up, Brandon will get me there, and you go home and take a rest."

All the party mood of Brandon just shut off after listening to Alyssa.

"Alyssa, do you know which part it is at least?" asked Joseph curiously.

"I'll share my live location," said Alyssa and nudged Brandon who stayed like a statue. Eventually the song "Kisi Disco Mein Jayee" ended.

They took their bike and moved. Joseph brushed his hair and texted Adina, "Alyssa and Brandon are risking their lives."

He sat on the bench and closed his eyes with stress.

Alyssa drove the bike to Kanahapuram and reached a resort. They entered the gate and had a walk to find a small restaurant, they went inside and asked for a man whom he bought the weed, a bar attender.

He came and greeted Brandon and they hugged each other. Alyssa gave a stern look at him.

"Hey man, that was some great stuff, where did you buy it?" Brandon asked.

"Hahaha, that is not your problem you enjoy the stuff," said the attendee.

"No, that is not the case, I'm getting this to Australia you know. I'm gonna make so much money from this. I have known the greatest dealers from various parts like Melbourne, Brisbane, Geelong, and even Hobart. So please consider and make me talk with the seller" Brandon spoke to him excitedly.

"No no that is out of my territory here I can't do that," said the attendee.

"Yooo, come on mate, I'm asking for the betterment for both of us and if you can know the stuff even you can make furthermore with me, and trust me, you know the business and I know the chemistry, errr umm sorry actually, in this case, you know the chemistry and I know the business," said Brandon.

Alyssa looked at him again with the same tight face. Attender said,

"Hey, I have heard this one somewhere..."

"Oh no, just leave that mate, just an extra push of fanaticism" Brandon exclaimed.

"Excuse me, are you guys going to take me there or not and can you please stop your shit talks..." Alyssa said after getting annoyed.

Brandon looked at Alyssa and thought about something,

The attendee called the reception of the bar and asked them to take to the place,

They were taken in a car to the other restaurant near the same place which is a bit older and running without any maintenance. Both entered inside and were asked to wait at the reception.

Chapter Eight

Meanwhile, Brandon asked Alyssa a doubt,

"Do shits even talk?"

"Ehnn…" Alyssa reacted disgustingly.

"Nope, you just told me and there I was thinking about that…" Brandon told in a husky voice,

"This is what a pure shit thinker thinks…" she lashed out at him in the same tone. Brandon calmly changed the topic,

"They don't serve Kangaroo curry here, I guess," he said.

She nodded at him and Brandon said, "Do you remember the days when the Australian government ordered us to have Kangaroo curry just because its population increased? Imagine what if it applied in India for the same reason.'

She whispered ironically, "If that happens with India, everyone should turn as Cannibals,"

"Umm, why?"

"Only population increase here is the human population," she said.

"No way! Jeez, this is real dark shit Alyssa," he said feeling awful.

Suddenly they heard the door screeching noise as Peter Durai entered. Brandon and Alyssa saw him. He looked very thin in muscles and wore a loose cotton shirt and a pant. He asked them to get into his office room.

"Hello Australians, what kinds of stuff do you like," he asked.

Alyssa still getting the flashes of the little girl she saw at the hospital and she was struggling a lot to be mentally present. Meanwhile, Brandon who was trying to keep her normal pushed her.

"Okay okay, I understand the need of the hour for madam, I'll give it. I have some amount of weed right under the table. You wish to smell it?" asked Peter Durai.

Brandon who felt anxious tried to pull back to normal and asked, "Mate, you're looking cool, how about your love life?"

Peter Durai just blinked.

Alyssa immediately asked Peter Durai,

"Mate, where do you get this stuff from?"

Peter Durai again blinked and felt like something was up with these Australians.

"So you are here just to get yourselves high or to more anything higher?"

"No, no we were just seeking for inspiration you know," said Alyssa hesitantly.

"People like you are the inspiration for so many youngsters here in India. Why don't we just take this feeling carried forward to Australia rather? Because you are so powerful look fantastic and you are already looking like a boss meanwhile you have some political support. I guess that too in this very young age," Brandon politely started talking with Peter Durai to build up a conversation.

His face changed a bit and he started observing both of them.

"Hello, mister Australian. You missed out on the thing in my powerful things, it is my caste that is driving me here powerfully." Peter Durai.

"Umm, but mate? How does this caste thing come into your political power strategy?" Brandon questioned him

"Caste is the most powerful thing for me to gain power and be powerful," said Peter Durai.

"Oof, but you are speaking good English I guess you got some college degrees and you own a big house restaurant, and jeez come on man…you got big money right. Are all these things smaller than your caste?" asked Brandon.

"Where you belong matters here the most than what belongs to you. And most importantly where you belong decides who you are and finally what are your belongings," Peter Durai said in a strong voice.

Alyssa nudged Brandon and said, "Haha that is cool. I guess we need to know more about the culture of India."

"May I see your Visa guys?" asked Peter Durai.

Alyssa said, "Oh yeah, I have it" and pretended like searching the bag. In the meantime, she texted Joseph and shared the live location.

"Alyssa, what are you searching for? Did you forget that our VISAs are with him for camera rent," said Brandon.

"Oh yeah, I'm sorry I forgot we gave our VISAs for taking a rental camera. I mean just for the precautionary measures they took those from us." Said Alyssa.

"May I know where is that rental shop?" asked Peter Durai.

Alyssa, compiling all the fake smiles she learned, said "I think, probably it is around the town somewhere near the beach. I couldn't remember the exact place. Maybe that is on the ground floor near the roadways here. I mean yeah, the roadways here in India are so aesthetically pleasing as well as soothing to drive out crazy but the traffic is hard unlike Australia, you know mate."

A complete silence prevailed among the three and Peter Durai stared at Alyssa with a cunning smile and said,

"Whom do you guys think you are, and whom do you think you are talking to?"

❋ ❋ ❋

Meanwhile, Adina was at the hospital crying, holding the phone. She received the text from Joseph. She wiped her face and rushed to the cop, Arockiyaraj, and showed the text she received from Joseph. That is a phone number and live location.

The location showed the exact coordinates.

Adina showed them to the cops and asked them not to involve the Australians who helped in this.

She signed at Arockiyaraj by having both hands in the way of worshiping.

He got the location coordinates and saw her face but didn't speak a word and asked two cops to stay there and he left the place.

✻   ✻   ✻

"Umm. Mister Durai, we were just randomly asking things. Didn't mean to hurt you. You must understand that we need stuff," said Alyssa.

Peter Durai asked his henchmen to lock the door of his office.

Brandon was shocked and Alyssa's face changed for the first time.

Peter then went to the corner of the room and picked up a sack of metal weapons. He pulled out a long-sized single piece of sword-like knife from it.

"Do you think you are smart enough to get things out here?" asked Peter.

"No, no we aren't smart. It is you, mate, you look fantastic and powerful. Violence is not the option mate," Brandon pleaded.

"I will not regret my killings and this is not new to me to destroy outsiders like you," said Peter.

"Mister Durai, please understand. We need Cannabis that's it," asked Alyssa.

"What is it with this Durai? Call me by my caste surname. Do you know what my caste surname is?" asked Peter, and he again raised his voice and said,

"Do you know what my caste surname is?"

Immediately, the door was knocked harder. He went to the door and opened it to see one of his henchmen standing with bruises on his face.

"What?" Peter was shocked to see newly appointed Police Inspector Arockiyaraj standing with the arrest warrant.

"It's you?" Peter was surprised more than shocked.

"Yeah me. Finally got the paper I wanted and also the evidence I needed. So shall we proceed?" asked Arockiyaraj.

Peter Durai looked at the Australians who refused to give an eye at Peter.

Arockiyaraj saw both Alyssa and Brandon closely and went away without uttering a word to them.

Arockiyaraj again nudged Peter to walk but he pushed firmly only to get himself held by the other two policemen.

He was taken into police custody, in the police jeep. He took his mobile and called his mentor, but he didn't pick up.

One of the henchmen ran towards him and said, "Anna they say he will not agree to our terms as he is not our guy."

Arockiyaraj came to him with the handcuff and arrested him. He took a sum of three hundred and fifty rupees from his pocket and kept it in Peter's pocket and saw his face. He then went to the front and sat in his seat,

Peter looked front to see his face in the rear mirror. His eyes turned into red cherry out of anger and Arockiyaraj adjusted it to see himself.

✻　✻　✻

Meanwhile, at the tea shop, Alyssa was having tea and Brandon argued with the tea master to play the song he played twenty minutes ago.

Joseph hugged Alyssa tightly and thanked her. Brandon won the battle with the tea master to play the song, "Kisi Disco Mein Jayees".

"Please don't smoke weed," he said to her.

"I don't have that in my pockets," she whispered.

"Where else?" asked Joseph.

Alyssa showed the pockets of Brandon who was still dancing for the song.

At the hospital, some cops cleared their way and advised Christopher Raj to warn his son. He also informed them that Peter Durai was arrested and not to worry again.

Adina went to the ICU ward and saw her brother's condition. Her father slowly regained some strength and asked Adina,

"Who's the one who helped us?"

Her face reflected the nervousness her body felt and stared at her father.

Her father kept on asking about the person who helped but she was unable to answer that and simply stared at her father in confusion.

Finally, after all the confusion, Joseph asked Alyssa and Brandon to come home for the first time,

"Is that you mate? That's insane... you hated us, I thought you just threw us away..." he said.

Joseph smiled and started "People come into our life and..."

"No no no wait, wait...It seems like you're going to start something cringe. I pretend I didn't hear that. Okay, we'll come home but make sure the Jesus photographs have some covers..."

"No, actually your rental time is over. I need to hand over your passports to you and you said you have work to do here, right? To go to some other place from here, I'll arrange that and say goodbye. We shall discuss that this evening...at my place?"

Alyssa also smiled and waved at Joseph who left the place.

Joseph after reaching home, received a text from Adina, "My father is asking about the person who helped us."

"Tell him, it's Alyssa," he replied.

"No way, if my father gets to know about her, it's over for me," she replied.

"Please tell her name. She will take care of it all," Joseph texted and closed the mobile to open the gate, then he found that the door was still locked and his mom was not back home.

He sat in the corridor for some time and heard his mom's anklet sound approaching his home. He immediately got up to see her and hugged her.

"Joseph, Joseph…what's wrong? What happened?" asked Jesintha.

Joseph inhaled and said, "This is a day to be remembered, Mom"

"What would that be? You would've roamed somewhere clicked natures and you must have praised yourself for better frames, isn't that? You self-obsessed kiddo," said Jesintha mockingly.

He smiled and they opened the house and he said,

"Ma, my friends are coming home this evening."

"Your friends, in this town? I thought all were going to various places," Jesintha asked.

"Not from this town," he hesitantly said.

"Where else from?" she asked.

"Friends from Australia…" he said.

* * *

Christopher Raj again asked about the person who helped them,

Adina came to her father and let him know by saying, "Pa, it's Alyssa, my friend."

* * *

Both Alyssa and Brandon reached their place and cleaned everything to vacate the place as their visa term was almost over.

Alyssa saw Joseph's camera, took that captured picture, and asked Brandon to stand near the window just to cover the Thiruvalluvar statue which was visible from their place. Brandon held his smile with a pose for one last picture in Kanyakumari.

Chapter Nine

Kaliyan found himself in a place where he could only see the mirage everywhere, and he wrapped a very thin toiled sack around his waist, which was about to get torn due to the scorching heat out there. He was only able to see those mirages which was giving him nightmares to look at. All he saw was the sun's heat and then soon he was not able to take a step forward holding the cloth he wrapped around.

He fell in the heat and he saw a girl standing alone alongside the mirages. He noticed that in his half-opened eyes and he immediately reacted to it. He instantly ran towards her and the girl, who was standing alone, wore a half saree only showing her back to Kaliyan. He approached her and suddenly he stopped and closed his ears, then closed his eyes. A large vulture-like creature appeared near him and started flapping its wings heavily around him. The heavy flapping sound increased and it gave him chills.

He endeavored to find courage within himself and opened his eyes to see the vulture shrink in size and went to sit on the shoulders of the mysterious girl. He was excited to see her and tapped on her shoulders. The vulture again started to flap its wings but this time he closed his ears sooner than before and eventually the vulture-like creature flew away. Then she slowly turned at him and all he saw was a faceless girl whose skull was damaged heavily and all those eyes nose and lips were damaged and rotten. He immediately shouted and opened his eyes to see him sharing the bed with Marthandan who was having soup behind him in the same room at the church.

He saw Valli nearer to him and also the Father who was also taken down by the thorn show of Marthandan and Kaliyan. Meanwhile, Kaliyan asked about VAO, only to find him above his head as he was made to lie down horizontally due to the lack of space inside. Valli took a cotton and gently treated the injuries and Kaliyan saw Marthandan who had minimal injuries among all, while the VAO received the heavier dose comparatively. Father Ben received something between mid and high and could stand and walk. Isabella who just finished her rituals for Jesus Christ whom she claims as Lord Krishna came out and said,

"When does the festival start? She is asking."

Father asked, 'Who is she?"

Melissa from inside replied, "Don't ask her about that and just answer her questions"

"No, it is getting too complicated and by now, we should have begun our festival. The time has come and I suggest we shouldn't be bothering about Moothakani anymore. Under the leadership of Isabella, we should be able to start our pooja for "Vadamala Bootham"."

From the moment Father said this, the entire room members felt an earthquake in their hearts for they didn't want to hear the name "Vadamala Bootham". It was said to be one of the most deadly Satanic creatures which was also worshiped by the people there mainly because it saved the forest and acted as the guard of the northern forest.

"Father, do we really need to get into that?"

Marthandan asked quietly from the bed.

"Yes, we need to prepare for the rituals accordingly."

"No, I don't want to be part of this. Better the festival shall get delayed" Kaliyan involved in the chat with a slightly tensed face and voice.

"No, we have no other option. We need to get it done within this Chithirai month."

Melissa opened the door of her room and entered to be a part of the conversation.

"I know she would love this. I know she would want this. How will she miss her son being present." Isabella blabbered looking at the Jesus statue.

Marthandan slowly got up from the bed and said, "Father if it is a ritual to be done for sure, then we should have to obey that."

"For whose sake? Father, you know how hard the ritual is," Kaliyan interrupted Marthandan.

"Enough. Shall I decide? I'm the VAO of the village. If you want everything to be fulfilled, you please act accordingly in favor of your village and throw away your ego and its clashes for God's sake."

Meanwhile, Mullan, who was sitting on the same bed as Marthandan, asked whom Isabella was referring to as "she" to which Marthandan asked him to remain silent and said, "Will tell you, now please stay quiet."

"We will meet on Friday. Until that, everyone please remain united and let peace be with you all." Everyone dispersed. Marthandan sneaked a look at Melissa and she didn't care as usual but this time he didn't turn back at all. At the same time, Valli carefully accompanied the injured Kaliyan to home. Marthandan was quite upset and he asked Mullan to arrange for a drink later that evening, and also he warned him to check the activities of Kaliyan regularly so that he could not go ahead in the Moothakani race.

On his way back home, Cinderella also known as Ponni came running in and tried to jump over Kaliyan. Immediately, Valli stopped her and asked her to wait.

"There is already someone waiting inside," said Cinderella.

It was Mani, who went to Thiruvananthapuram had come back, and waited to meet Kaliyan, but he was shocked to see the injuries on his face and asked about it.

"I'll explain and before that, where were you? I searched for you at some crucial moments but you were missing at Isabella's."

"Ayoo chetta, I went to get my passport from Thiruvananthapuram. I told you already, right? What was it for? What happened? Is everything okay?"

"Does my face look okay?"

"No."

"But I'm okay," Kaliyan asked him to move and went inside. Meanwhile, Cinderella nudged Mani about the chocolates, and he patiently answered. Suddenly the little kid took his bag and ran into the other room to find the chocolates that Mani bought. He ran towards her as well and Valli followed him.

In the room after giving chocolates to Cinderella, Mani asked Valli,

"Valli-ichi, may I ask you one thing?" Valli nodded,

"What is so wrong with that guy Marthandan? Why is he spitting venom at Kaliyan brother all the time, and he hates himself? What is the issue between them? I have seen them as foes all my life…but many say they were good friends when they were young and they both did so many good deeds for Kanikar? Can you explain?"

"They are foes. That is what people of your generation would have known. Even though I didn't belong to their generation, I had seen them together when I was small. There was something else that was between their bond. It was nineteen years ago…" Valli started to explain the backstory of Marthandan and Kaliyan.

Nineteen years ago, in the mid-2000s, on a fine summer evening in the dense forest of Neyyar, young Kaliyan and Marthandan went honey hunting which was the sole occupation of Kanikar. They both shared a great bond. They both played together and were together in all their life events. Their main hobby was honey hunting and they were involved in that immensely.

On that evening, after returning from the forests they stopped at Dravyapara and both worshipped their deities and started walking around. They were stopped by an old man who ran on the slope of the village panting heavily.

"Kaliya…Marthandaa…they have come again…"

Both's face changed and they rushed back into the village center at Sasthan temple. They were shocked to see a group of villagers arguing with some people who seemed like official officers. Marthandan and Kaliyan went closer and listened to the problem. It was all about the construction of valley view resorts as the sub-village of Amboori, where the Kanikars live has one of the most beautiful valleys and viewpoints in the country. Several NGOs and private landlords were keen on buying that land but the chieftains of the Kanikar tribes didn't allow them ever. However, the Kanikars were without the Moothakani, as John the Moothakani died a year ago, so the officials and the landlords were keen on capturing the land of the Tribes,

Kaliyan and Marthandan knew the issue and looked at each other. Amidst the arguments, Marthandan ran to the other side to reach the vehicles of the officials, and Kaliyan emoted to the officials.

"Hello sir, we are not just a random hill tribe. We are the natives, we built this mountain, we cultivated every crop of it and they belong to our tribe and we don't spare any chance for outsiders to occupy our precious place."

"Who are you to tell this? Are you their chieftain?" asked one of the officers. Suddenly they heard a blast and they turned to see Marthandan standing on top of a car and having broken the windshield.

"Eda Kaliyaa…is this sound enough?"

"No, not audible enough to create the tension," Kaliyan replied from there.

Marthandan then broke the top of the car with the same iron rod.

On seeing this, the official members tried to threaten Kaliyan.

"I'll file a complaint against you. You are gonna regret this."

"Okay, I'm ready. Before that please be ready to face the issue about the deer hunting you did yesterday. We have witnesses for that…"

"Witness? Whom?"

"The girl who showed you the deer, the little kiddo Valli."

Ten-year-old Valli was laughing at the official.

"We just smashed your car, and you have another to go down the hill. But if you continue to mess up, the other car will be gone. You need to trespass the mountain and you will be heartily welcomed by the cheetahs, leopards, and some Tigers too. It's good for you to do as we say," Kaliyan gave back the warning,

They took to their heels and Marthandan came down running to Kaliyan and lifted him on his shoulders and boasted

"We just saw the glimpse of our new chieftain, the new Moothakani…" and the crowd joined.

Meanwhile, near the Dravyapara, a group of hornbills were sitting on a cliff. Nearby, a girl in her late teens was sitting and throwing barns of rice at the birds. Suddenly, a hornbill came near her, whose nose looked like a horn, and also the national bird of the state Kerala. The girl took the bird in her palms and looked at it straight to face. She blew from her mouth and the bird started to spread its wings and flapped heavily. The sound of those birds' flaps made her feel so emotional and personal and they flew away. Eventually, the group of birds started to fly as well. It went past the Dravyapara cliff and flew happily. The girl's eyes bloomed and her pupils went bigger and she murmured to none but herself.

"I'll join to fly with you one day. I should remember I have wings too…"

Ponni, a girl from Amboori, daughter of Chokkan and Thadadhagai, was from the family which was the authority of Sasthan temple and its worship. Her father used to navigate people before their harvesting and the people believed that he predicted the good and bad for the day and the path they take every day.

The girl who loved nature was always seen near the hornbills at the cliff. She loved to see them flap their wings and listen to those. She was the most attractive girl in the village and was loved and admired by many people.

After sending off the birds at the cliff, she was greeted by her friend on her way back home.

"Hey Ponni, have you sent off the birds? What did they say?" her friend asked.

"It said that they will take me to the west where the sun sets next time and for that I need to have wings…" Ponni replied.

"Your wings? For that, you need to grab permission from our New Moothakani to be."

"Who's that?"

"Your long-time love interest, Kaliyan…"

Ponni's pupils again lit up when she heard the name Kaliyan and she rushed to Sasthan temple and saw her parents involved in the temple works. She greeted them on her way and rushed to the center of the village but she still couldn't find Kaliyan.

She ran for quite a few kilometers and her body was wrenched in sweat. She wore a half sari and tied it up and was given a tender coconut from a small girl Valli. She smiled at the girl and asked,

"Where is the Moothakani of the town?"

Little girl Valli explained everything that happened a few hours ago and Ponni realized why they called Kaliyan, the new Moothakani of the town. She saw the time and it was almost evening. She thought of something and realized where Kaliyan would be. She immediately washed her face and ran to the Amboori mainland bus stop. She removed the bindi on her forehead when the bus arrived which was on route between Neyyar Dam and Vellarada village.

She boarded the bus to see Melissa who was in her early twenties, sitting at the first seat near the door. She took the seat next to her and smiled at her.

"Enda ponnu Melissa ichi, how are you? I missed your beautiful eyes and how's your typewriting class going," Ponni asked.

"Ohh Ponni is here! What a pleasant sight! Yeah, it is going good. Have your horn bills found their way?" Melissa asked.

"Hmm, but another male bird is missing. I may suspect that the bird is now flying in a bus with his friend bird to see a mockingbird travel in her signature seat near the door…"

"Mockingbird? Me?" Melissa furiously rolled her bally eyes at her,

"Yeah, you are the mockingbird of Marthandan etta, right?

"Did he tell you?"

"Pch."

Ponni responded hypothetically. Melissa turned back to the last seat and could see no one. Simultaneously, a hand tapped on Ponni's shoulders. She turned to see her lover Kaliyan standing and staring at her. Her pupils once again widened, and she smiled at Kaliyan.

"Welcome, the new Moothakani of the tribe, Mr.Kaliyan…"

He suddenly closed her mouth and asked her not to shout.

"Who told you these?"

"I have an informer…"

Meanwhile, Melissa was upset with Marthandan for not turning up. She said to Ponni in distress.

"Ponni, come and sit there is nothing to do with men now,"

Kaliyan understood why Melissa was flaming in anger and he whistled as a signal to Marthandan who was hiding behind. He ran in to climb to the front door of the bus and smiled at Melissa.

She suddenly got scared and grabbed Ponni's hands.

Kaliyan whispered near Ponni's ears, "He is going to confess."

"How many spells man?" Ponni asked.

"Not going to last long," told Kaliyan

Marthandan got on the bus and whispered something in Kaliyan's ears. Ponni and Melissa looked at each other and then Kaliyan said,

"He's asking all of us to come to Drvayapara Cliff tomorrow as the bus is fully crowded.' Having said that he saw the half-empty bus and only a few were sitting in the seat.

❋ ❋ ❋

At Dravyapara, Ponni and Kaliyan were sitting near the cliff and Ponni and Melissa were sitting near a rock and viewing one of the most beautiful scenes of Kerala. Marthandan was waiting near her to confess his love for her.

"How's your day?" Kaliyan asked.

"It is as good as it gets to rest my head on your shoulders…" Ponni replied.

On hearing this Marthandan was shocked and said,

"Wish I had this much romance left in my mind…"

"We are not so romantic than what you bought for her from the town…" said Kaliyan.

"Shhhh…" Marthandan asked him to be silent. He held the gift in his pocket and then approached Melissa who was busy hazing at the clouds.

"Clouds? As good as your hair…" Marthandan started it. The couple stopped their romance and paid attention.

She changed her look to the blue sky,

"Sky…as vast as your forehead…"

She then got a little bit annoyed and looked at the leaves of the plants near her,

"Leaves? As good as your eyelashes…"

She got annoyed even more and looked down at the rock,

"Rock…? Hmmm" he started thinking and took some time and the couple was also keen to hear what he was going to deliver. Melissa lost interest and decided to change her look, but Marthandan was spot on with that,

"Rock…? As good as your heart…" He said…

Both Ponni and Kaliyan busted out in laughter and Melissa joined them lately and Marthandan got embarrassed. Immediately, they heard the church bell and Melissa suddenly got up and packed her bag, bid bye to Ponni and Kaliyan. She again turned at Marthandan and smiled at him and rushed back to the village.

On seeing her smile, he was so happy and said,

"Eda Kaliya…did you see her smile at me? Did you notice that? It was like the exact first drop of monsoon in June…it wiped away all my dryness…"

"Ayoo chetta…how could you tell this? You were very off to her…" Ponni asked.

"This wasn't planned, I just uttered what my heart said…"

"Do the same when you meet her next time," Kaliyan said, and Marthandan decided to leave and asked about the couple. But they were keen on having moments with horn bills hitting the cliff.

At the church, as the bell rang, a younger Father Ben, who wore a safari on top and a pant at the bottom, called all the devotees of the church, including Melissa. He gathered them for the meeting which was arranged in the church as it was time for the people of Kanikar to do the Sasthan festival, and also it was the duty of the Church people to celebrate Palli festival. For that, they need to assign someone willing to devote themselves to God, just like Father Ben did. The meeting took place that evening in the church.

Father started, "May our lord bless us in this calm evening of the village…let the glory of Jesus Christ be upon us."

The prayer started and the rest of the people joined Father.

"We were about to devote someone to god. With all due respect to her decision, we suggest Ms. Melissa devote herself to Jesus Christ as a Nun sister of this village and also to promote Jesus Christ outside of this church and also should be proud of the community of Kanikar, Amen. " Father finished his speech and the crowd joined. Isabella almost kissed Melissa on her forehead but Melissa was in shell shock and was still processing the message she got a few minutes earlier.

"I think Melissa needs time to process, maybe a day?" asked Isabella.

"Do you?" Father asked and Melissa replied nothing and looked at the statue of Jesus Christ.

"Alright, Melissa. We will have our community meeting where the heads of the families will come and throw their scarves for the Sasthan festival. Before that, you need to make a decision. There is a reason why I'm asking. You were born and brought up in this church and you have already devoted yourself through your mind and you had studied your college in Idukki missionary. It is all from this church and I guess you don't know anyone other than Jesus Christ. You don't have your parents either, and I don't think any man is behind you in this village. So you should take up this as it would affect none…" said Father Ben.

"Affect none…? But what about me?" Melissa asked herself in her mind. Isabella suddenly wiped the tears of Melissa and said,

"See Ben, she has already started to shed tears for people!" and then the church dispersed. But Melissa didn't. She kneeled in front of Jesus, looked at the statue keenly, and spoke with her hard-hitting eyes. At one stage, she decided to close her eyes to see whether she was seeing the crucifixion of Jesus. She only heard Marthandan saying,

"Rock…? As hard your heart…" She immediately opened her eyes and started sobbing without a single noise from her throat. She was taking herself into a state of trance through her mind as she wasn't able to concentrate on Jesus. All she could see and sense was Marthandan and his love for her.

Chapter Ten

Meanwhile, the same evening, watching the sun set at the west, both Kaliyan and Ponni were inviting the horn bills one by. The birds arrived in groups. Initially, Kaliyan hesitated to touch the bird but after his girlfriend insisted, he lost fear and touched the bird which had big horned like nose.

"Why are you so obsessed with this bird?" he asked her.

"Have you looked at their wings and feathers? Have you ever listened to them flap those wings? And have you ever longed for the sound of those flaps? You wouldn't because I don't think you have a desire to fly like them as you are already flying like a champ…"

He smiled and asked, "Why do you want to fly?"

Ponni looked at him closely and said,

"I don't know my dearest. I have never seen a woman flying, of course, I didn't see a man fly. But somehow you know, women of our tribe, our community, even in churches, women are always treated as the prominent asset of culture, pride, and dignity. All these were manipulated and laid upon them with respect to a man. I don't know why…and had always wondered how the women who studied a lot would go through this. Women in cities and towns? I really have no idea, and you know what?

The shame and dignity only offer pride in the body of a woman. If some woman is being stripped off or raped, she will suffer more than the man who pushed her to that. I always wished for women to have wings to fly…to fly out of their families, their house, their villages, their country and I have always been fascinated to have wings to fly out of the world."

He was mesmerized by her words, and he was admiring her like a statue. She shook him and he eventually coughed and the hornbills got ready to fly as well. Then Ponni insisted he listen to the sound of the birds flapping. He lent his keen ears to the heavy sound of hornbills flying away from the cliff. As the sun set, it painted the sky orange and the hornbills flew like the artist splashed some black paint over the sky.

As it got even more cooler and darker which also sent off the hornbills, Ponni wanted to go back home,

"A few more minutes? As we have still some orange left…" he asked.

Ponni hesitated first but remembered their motto as to see the sunsets completely and not leave in between. She came back to her position,

"When will my horn bill have its wings?" he again asked. Ponni again looked him in the eyes and said,

"On the day when this bird gets married to you…"

"So do you think, getting married is the only option we have?"

"What else do you think?" she exclaimed.

"Something holier than that?"

"Holier than marriage? That means? We weren't taught that it's something holier than a marriage."

They both knew what they wanted but somehow they were so hesitant on initiating things. He moved further away from her and she followed him with heavy breaths. But then she moved away from him and he pulled her back. The hesitation saga continued only until the sun set completely.

As darker it got, they both came closer and closer. They both believed that the night and the darkness will only help them to initiate further without seeing each other's face and without confessing the first touch of love. The darkness helped them to lose their shyness and the hesitations of the first move.

They both collided like the rain clouds and eventually, the rain poured. The moon came in as the spectator along with some fellow celestial objects as the witness of their collision. The leaves began to blush seeing them make love even in that dark night.

✳ ✳ ✳

The next morning, the entire village gathered at Isabella's for the discussion of the Sasthan ritual. All those years, it was Isabella who did the ritual of walking alone in the nude to feed Vadamala bootham and Vettikadu pei. But as the condition got worse than normal for her due to aging, she wasn't offered this time and she also made her devotions more towards Lord Krishna and Jesus Christ.

Father Ben and some headmen of the village gathered, and all the heads of the families were present at the meeting. Marthandan came with his father Kanthan with the scarf. Ponni's parents came and Kaliyan came with the scarf as he only had his mother at home. Both Marthandan and Kaliyan waved at each other and smiled with eyebrows. Father Ben and the sun chieftains of the village explained the ritual.

"All the heads of the families must tell their opinion about the Sasthan ritual, it is all about a woman of chaste who should replicate our deity should walk around our tribal streets and should cross the Dravyapara and feed Vadamala bootham and Vettikadu pei. For this eligibility, that woman should be untouched by their family's men for at least seven days before the walk. This meeting is held to let whoever doesn't want their family to be involved in this to know that they can put your scarf down as a sign of unwillingness..."

Everyone from the crowd threw their scarf immediately. Marthandan's father Kanthan threw it and almost every family threw the scarves in. Kaliyan was waiting for his turn to throw down, but he saw Ponni's father Chokkan didn't throw down his scarf. He was panicking as he would bring Ponni to the scene as he had already been with Sasthan temple and stuff. He waited for him to throw down but he didn't. Finally, he tied up his scarf tightly as a sign of allowing his family lady, who was Ponni for the ritual. The entire crowd was buzzing around and Kaliyan was in shock. His turn came and his hands were shaking. He was imagining her girlfriend walking nude in the town at night and he knew that his girlfriend was more sensitive about these issues. But he cannot confess to the entire village that he had sex with her. He hadn't got any guts to confess what he did which could have saved her from the ritual.

He finally threw his scarf and the meeting ended. Marthandan called him and asked about his anxiousness. He explained the whole thing and he told him that he wanted to meet Ponni.

Back in home, she was crying hard and pulled down all the utensils from the shelf. Her parents were forcing her to accept.

"Moley, it is for our tribe and the God. You will be equally treated and seen as our deity who lives in Dravyapara." Ponni's father Chokkan tried to convince her.

"What about me? I myself am superior to all of your Gods. I should save my body. I should save my life. Why should I do this?" asked Ponni.

She was suddenly slapped by her mother Thadadhagai and Ponni was shocked again to hear her say,

"You're a woman and you should act accordingly."

"Maa, for what I should act accordingly? I never expected a woman to say this ma. Our entire community worships the Goddess as a deity and we all expect a woman not to speak against these. For all the sake of that nude woman who came and flashed a thousand years ago? I wouldn't do it for her."

She was slapped again by her father and he locked her in the room and came out.

At Church, Melissa and her churchmates were lying together in a room. She couldn't even get a wink of sleep as the people around her were talking about the benefits of being a nun and how lucky Melissa was to get selected.

"Hey Melissa, it's true when Father said that you are blessed among the women. Remember the holiness of Virgin Mary? She gave birth to Jesus Christ with all holiness, and she will shower you with all the love."

"But did anyone ask Mary if she was okay to give birth to Jesus?" Melissa asked herself in her mind and closed her eyes to see only Marthandan smiling innocently at her on the bus, on the road, and sometimes in the church.

The next evening, Kaliyan was sitting alone at the Dravyapara cliff and a single horn bill arrived at the cliff and searched for their friend Ponni. Soon the group came in and went disappointedly without seeing Ponni. He was paying attention to those flaps.

Marthandan was roaming around the village with his gift looking for Melissa but she wasn't seen outside the church or anywhere else since that meeting.

Meanwhile, at her house, Ponni was crying desperately as she wanted to meet Kaliyan and avoid the ritual at any cost. Her father along with some villagers were getting their home ready for the Sasthan Pooja. They invited Isabella to their house and she felicitated the occasion with some prayers and bhajans.

That night was set for the biggest turnaround ritual of the village. Villagers were seen cooking early evening as there shouldn't be anyone outside the village as per the rules during the ritual. There would only be the selected girl, Ponni, who would be walking alone around the streets and cross Drayapara to offer the food, fruits, and crops to Vadamala bootham and Vettikadu pei. Ponni was inching to meet Kaliyan at any cost but she was denied forcefully. Meanwhile, Marthandan was still waiting for Melissa to come out of the church but she didn't turn up.

"Ohh Marthanda-etta? You're too here to congratulate her alle?" said a friend of Melissa who was also a member of the Church and waved at Marthandan.

Marthandan wasn't sure what was she talking about. So he clarified and his brains acted quickly to attain trauma as he would be seeing her girl as a nun. He reacted immediately and told her that he wanted to meet Melissa. He entered the church and waited for her to come but she was very clear that as she was to be selected as the nun and so until the time, she would not come out of the church. He was very much disappointed and couldn't stop his tears. He was shell-shocked by this and he recalled all the childhood memories he had with her.

The evening dusk filled the streets of Amboori at Chithirai Street. Marthandan along with his street mate Mullan, met Kaliyan at their favorite tree shed. Marthandan told everything to him and Kaliyan was also worried about the decision taken by the father.

"Da, shall we take this to Father?" Kaliyan asked.

"How can we? Who am I? What was I doing all these days? How can he give her to me? He hardly speaks to me…

He never understands what I'm going through now. It's up to one and only person." he said.

"Who?"

"Melissa. She has to answer this and I need to ask at least one time whether she has feelings for me or not. I need to give this and for that, I need to meet her but how can I within tomorrow?"

Kaliyan thought of an idea and said,

"Tonight?"

"Ehh?"

"Yeah, tonight is the only option. Only Ponni would be roaming in the village and no one dares to step out of their houses. You go and meet her and ask the whole thing in front of Jesus."

Mullan said, "Da, your idea is good…but how can I see her now?"

"Shall we go for the evening prayer?" Kaliyan asked and they both went to church for the evening prayer. They saw Melissa at the corner of the church singing gospel songs. Marthandan took out the piece of paper he had where he wrote, "At 12.30 A.M. Today". He went near by the Mary statue where there was a hundi where the devotees pour in their applications to Jesus. He pretended that he did pour that piece of paper but gave it to Melissa and moved away. She read that.

Immediately Marthandan ran to Kaliyan and hugged him. Kaliyan's mind was off as he was thinking about Ponni. He understood that and he asked him to meet her at Isabella before the ritual.

At Isabella's, a few men and several women were present to felicitate the function of Sasthan pooja, which they celebrate with some holiness. Also, they were keen on ending their fast. Both Kaliyan and Marthandan reached there by their cycle and Kaliyan was tensed about the crowd at Isabella's.

Inside the house, Ponni was bathed with turmeric powder and she was cleansed with it. She was given a towel to wrap around her for the evening and she was asked to unwrap the cloth exactly at midnight. She came out and she was felicitated by the villagers. Some called her the exact reincarnation of their deity. Many highly aged people came in and touched the feet of Ponni which made her feel embarrassed. Kaliyan used this opportunity to touch her feet and said,

"Enda ponnu mole Ponni, be brave and we will leave the village tomorrow. They are never going to find us. You are going to fly as high as you can. I'll be waiting for you in the dawn at the cliff along with your horn bills…come back."

Ponni closed her eyes and cried inside but ultimately received the courage to do this. She took some time and finally opened her furious eyes and the villagers had gone wild of seeing her as their deity.

❋ ❋ ❋

The night has come. Kaliyan's mother locked him in a room as he would try to do anything on the D-day's night.

He was thinking about his love. Marthandan, on the other hand, waited for the village to lock itself down to meet his girl. Melissa who lost her sleep in the church due to Marthandan's bit of notice was blinking her eyes at the starry night like the stars.

Ponni uncovered her body. Isabella took her out of the house, and the entire night was darker than pitch black. The village was shut down. No one was outside their houses. She was given the pooja stuff and she started her way to Dravyapara. On her way, she stopped at a place. She heard some leaves move in the forest. She immediately tried to hide her nude body with a leaf nearby but realized that no man from the village would have the guts to enter the pitch-black Dravyapara forest road. But she still sensed something and focused towards the sound and literally got shocked to see a fox eating a bunny which was hunted by some other animal. She was about to shout but closed her eyes in fear and suddenly opened it to see none there. That night gave some eerie illusions to Ponni, and it continued further on her way.

She again stopped at the sound of a crying woman and later found out that was also happened to be her illusion only adding up much more drama as she saw a woman sitting on the mid of the road. She boosted up some courage within herself and went closer to her. That woman didn't respond, then Ponni decided to close her eyes just to make this illusion go but that night the trick didn't work. The woman was still sitting down on the road and Ponni decided to move further away crossing the woman without bothering her. But all of a sudden, the woman started laughing and Ponni heard that vigorous laugh of her. But she didn't turn first. Then the laugh continued but she then turned to see none. She somehow managed to reach Dravyapara and crossed the forest to give the feast for Vadamala Bootham and Vettikaadu pei.

* * *

Meanwhile, at the church, Melissa was roaming in the church hall waiting for Marthandan to show up. It was the mid of the night and there were no one in the church. The empty arena spoke a million words to Melissa. It was so empty and that silence was the toughest sound she had ever listened to in her entire life. Marthandan's shadow from a single light at the door slowly hit Melissa. The silence broke as Melissa's teardrop made the sound of an earthquake in Marthandan's ears. Both their eyes met each other and spoke nothing that time. But he gave the gift which was wrapped in polyester paper and she grabbed that and opened it to see a pair of Jhumkas, her eyes lit up in joy and the very next second she was struck by agony. She didn't speak at all. He on the other hand uttered very few words.

"Melissa, I'm none to you as of now. But I hope you're none to Jesus as well as of now. You may never know how much you mean to me and how I lived with you and how I'm living with you in my life. I never tasted honey without thinking about you. I never saw the moon without thinking of you. I never laughed without remembering you. You had been my breath, you will always be my breath. I even imagined marrying you at this same church. But only God plans everything not humans. Consider this as my first and last gift. If you turn up with this tomorrow morning, I will grab your hand and take you to the father and ask for our marriage. But if you didn't, I will leave you to Jesus and will never come back again."

Melissa's hormones drifted in all possible ways and her emotions swung way harder than the pendulum. She wasn't able to answer Marthandan or neglect him. She bit her tongue and controlled all her feelings and looked at him who was walking away from the church. She couldn't even shout or call him as the entire village was locked down. She then rushed to him and he sensed her coming. He turned back to see Melissa standing right behind him. It was the all-time closest call between them. Marthandan had seen his moon positioned itself in its closest orbit. Both looked into their eyes and their look got even deeper. Melissa's breath aroused him and his eyes claimed her to break all the rules she had written for herself.

The pumping energy of her took even harder and she breathed heavily. The smell of her breath entered him and he was about to lose every other thing in his world. He inhaled it and tightly closed her eyes. She took a step back and saw him with a smile and spoke nothing. She only showed the Jhumkas and shadow hanged those in her ears under the single door light and he had just witnessed a new full moon in a new moon day.

❋ ❋ ❋

The next morning, the dawn was about to rise slowly from the east, Isabella was waiting for Ponni. She came along with the sun and Isabella greeted her and carried her in arms. She conducted a final pooja, then she checked her body and found a wound on her thighs. She immediately ran to her pooja room and prayed in her language to Lord Krishna and Lord Jesus Christ. Ponni was crying in pain and she herself made some leaves as the remedy to the wounds then Isabella found that her vagina was also wounded as it was bleeding. She at once rang the bell and called up the entire village.

The whole village panicked that something had happened that shouldn't have happened. A woman who went for Sasthan pooja should come back in the morning without any wounds on her body even by the animals. That was why they always select virgin girls as having sex should have got semen remains on their vagina, which might attract the female ghosts in the forest. Meanwhile, Kaliyan was waiting at the cliff of Dravyapara as he promised with respect to the plan to elope.

Ponni was standing in front of the village, and the entire village was told that she was wounded and something had happened at night.

"Our deity lives in the vagina of the woman which is wounded now." said a voice from the crowd.

"No one knows…what consequences are waiting for us."

"It's her shame, she had to be properly clean and pure. She ditched our place, she ditched our holiness."

"Our deity is the holiest woman, and we made a mistake by sending this dirtiest female. That is why she was wounded, the God's plan."

The entire village was going wild at Ponni and she was helplessly standing in front, only to add to the suffering. Her father Chokkan came in and started scolding her and slut shamed her straight on her face.

"What did you do? What happened last night?" he asked.

Ponni didn't tell anything and she wimped looking at her father. Then he whopped her with the rope he had and swore on her and completely slut shamed her in front of the village. He held her hair and spitted on her face and acted vigorously in front of everybody. Then the people slowly moved away. He kicked her in the stomach and left the place.

She was left strangled on the road lying down without anyone's help and Isabella came to her and said,

"That shouldn't have happened my dear."

Ponni could not bear the pain in her body and the mind. The dawn spread completely and the sun was boiling on top to see her lying on the ground like a womb in the uterus her hair was scattered along and her tears paved the way for a new running stream in the village. She can't even move her knees and her father kicked her on the knees. She was helplessly lost on the road.

At the church, without knowing all those dramas, Melissa took a bath and got ready with her jhumkas. She got dressed in a peach color top with black a skirt. She was waiting for Marthandan, looking at the church door from the morning but he didn't arrive. Fathen Ben arrived to the church with the long white gown for the first time and he asked the workers about the ceremony. Melissa had very few minutes left in her life to decide the path.

Suddenly, the church was informed about the tragedy that happened to Ponni. Father rushed to the spot. Melissa on hearing the news felt shattered and was confused about what must have happened in the night. She finally decided to step out of church to meet Marthandan at his house.

The church people reached the spot but they couldn't find Ponni.

At Dravyapara cliff, Kaliyan who was still waiting for her, finally heard the sound of the anklets. He confirmed that it was Ponni and reached out to invite her but he was painfully dumbfounded to see her face and her devastated body wounds. He immediately hugged her and she was screaming out louder in pain. But her vocals didn't help her much with sound. He got no clue, but he understand the wrong that was happened to her.

"Kaliya…am I a slut?" she muttered in pain.

He grabbed her face looked deeper into her eyes and asked her,

"What did happen?"

Ponni suddenly got furious and moved further away from him. She was acting weirdly and he wasn't sure what he must do. Ponni attained the state of trance and acted vigorously in front of him. She took off the single cloth she was wrapped around and made herself nude.

"Kaliya…look at me, this is me…they were right? The semen remains in our vagina made me like this. The ghosts attacked me but it mustn't be a female ghost. A woman cannot hurt another woman, Kaliya. I was called a bitch and a slut. I wish I hadn't dreamed about myself. I should have gone with the timid mindset of cultured men and women. I shouldn't have wished for wings, even though knowing I couldn't fly…only a horn bill should have wings and rights to fly across not a woman."

He again hugged her and kissed all over her head and consoled her with his love. But he didn't know that she was on the verge of losing her sanity. She was blinking and saw around the cliff. Kaliyan asked her,

"Ponni, shall we go to some other place? Shall we start a new life? Let us leave this place."

She didn't listen to him and saw the edge of the cliff where a hornbill flew over it. She smiled at it. She moved away from Kaliyan and ran to the bird. She was smiling at the bird and she saw the bird face to face Kaliyan was watching her and was relieved that she might get back to normal after seeing her favorite bird.

Ponni then caressed the wings and feathers of the bird. The heavy flapping sound of the wings hit Kaliyan's ears. She inhaled the smell of that bird and its feathers and imagined herself as the hornbill. She had got her imaginary wings from her limbs and suddenly her eyes lit up and said,

"Let me have my wings." She shouted at Kaliyan.

"Kaliya, I have got what I wanted. Let me fly along with this bird. I'll come back to see you soon."

In a fraction of a second, she flew from the cliff along with the bird. The bird flew away and the poor lady fell from the cliff even before Kaliyan reacted. She fell pretending that she could fly. He ran to the edge of the cliff to see Ponni falling. He couldn't believe his eyes and all he was able to hear was the flapping of the birds. The sound increased, the intensity grew higher, and the sound was eerier than that entire previous night.

✳ ✳ ✳

At Marthandan's, he and Mullan were boozing and Marthandan's face wasn't as cool and innocent as before. Mullan seemed forcing him to drink. They heard the door knock.

It was Kaliyan, who was shattered and slanted on the door. They were shocked and grabbed him inside. They shook him and cleaned his face with water. Kaliyan asked,

"Eda Marthanda…what did you do to her last night?"

Marthandan's eyes raised in misery and Mullan saw him as well.

"Da…What are you asking about?" Marthandan curiously asked back.

"Ponni is dead, I saw her falling down the cliff…"

Marthandan slipped down on the floor on hearing the news and Mullan was also shocked. Marthandan started to cry and he was more anxious and tense than Kaliyan. Suddenly Kaliyan slapped him and asked,

"Why did you do this to her? You were the only one man who was outside in this entire village…why did you do this?"

"No, I didn't…I don't know what happened," he uttered the truth.

"So, why haven't you come to see me at the cliff? What made you booze this much earlier in the morning? Tell me my dear friend," he was raging on, especially by the pain he couldn't handle.

Marthandan got angry and pushed him away and said,

"Da Kaliya…stop thinking like a brat. I'm repeating I didn't do anything to her…she called me "cheta" ra…she is like my sis…" before even completing, Marthandan was given a heavy blow on the face by Kaliyan. Mullan came in between,

"Eda…what is wrong with you? Whatever happened is happened but how come you are blaming him? I got it…he is the only other candidate for Moothakani post other than you. To be unopposed you are playing the blame game, alle?"

Kaliyan was stunned and spit on the floor and grabbed onto the knowledge that they both were high on alcohol.

"Eda…Marthanda, my Ponni is gone, and you guys are talking about the post?"

Marthandan who was high, furiously got up and bashed him,

"Da…yeah, I wanted to be Moothakani but you were the only interruption. Please get off from it and I know nothing about Ponni."

In a heavy drunken state with his faltering legs, he pushed away Kaliyan out of his house. He opened the door to see Melissa standing with the peach color top and wearing the jhumkas on her ears. She didn't see his face but she heard what they were talking inside. Her face turned pink and she couldn't believe what was happening. She wasn't sure what must have happened to Ponni but she also knew that Marthandan was the only man who was outside last night.

The drunken Marthandan saw Melissa and didn't react accordingly. He saw her closely and tried to tell something. He suddenly worn out and hit the ground. He was taken inside by Mullan.

Marthandan was lying down on the floor, and he opened his eyes partially and he saw a huge snake come out of his nose. He saw it go by and he couldn't do anything but close his eyes. He did and opened back to see the snake turn back at him and saw face to face and bit him the next second.

Immediately, the water splashed on his face Mullan helped him to open his eyes fully to realize that all those were his hallucinations.

"Edo, Marthanda…at least now tell me, what happened last night?" Mullan asked.

Marthandan didn't say anything but shook his head.

Melissa came back to church, and kneeled down to Jesus Christ and took off her jhumkas and threw it in the ditch. She wore a white sari and removed all her face powder she worn in the morning.

Kaliyan came back home and fainted down on the floor near his Mother. He was made to lay down on his mother's lap and he cried heavily with fear. But he didn't turn up to the village as he didn't want to spoil Ponni's name after her death. He decided to dump his love story within him.

He then started to hear the sound of the birds flapping in his ears. He could not close his eyes, all he could see was Ponni smiling eerily towards him and flying with her wings off the cliff. The scenes were repeating within him and he closed his ears tightly with his palm to stop the sound but he couldn't. The eternal trauma hit Kaliyan.

In a few hours, the church people went and saw Ponni's body being scattered all over into pieces down the valley. They collected it and Father Ben gave it to their parents who weren't ready to accept it. The little girl Valli saw all these at Isabella's and she came in and was ready to accept her body.

"Ponni ichi?" asked the little girl Valli.

At present, Valli wiped tears while uttering the name, "Ponni-ichi". She confessed everything she had known as the child and also said why Kaliyan had been concerning Valli.

After listening to it, Mani was saddened about Ponni and asked about her parents. Valli replied,

"They left the place some years later…and it was the last time that pooja happened and no other festivals were conducted even for our church. Hmm, it has been nineteen long years."

"Valli, please spare me a minute and could you come here?" Kaliyan called her from his room.

Valli was shocked to hear him utter her name and so she got super excited to get to him. But she wasn't showing it on her face but she sped up.

"Valli-ichi, what would have exactly happened on that night in the forest beyond Dravyapara? Are there really Vadamala bootham and Vettikadu pei living? What would have hurt Ponni-ichi?" Mani asked.

"To know what happened, Marthandan has to break his silence…"

"But anyhow he must be telling what he saw or what he knew, but to know about the truth?"

"For the truth, only Ponni-ichi has to fly back to the cliff and confess to us," Valli replied and moved away.

Chapter Eleven

"You may not like the way I react or behave but you know what I must be going through, and eventually I know what you are going through as well. Never complain about your situation. It may change and if you lose yourself we cannot bring that back."

Valli wasn't sure why Kaliyan was talking about this and she did nothing and stared at him. He fell slowly on the bed and asked Valli to stay as he was feeling very lonely. Valli also took the hot water from the kitchen and gave it to him.

Kaliyan slowly looked her in the eyes which were sharper and hotter than the hot water he held. He turned aside immediately and he couldn't bear what he saw. She decided to leave the room and walked away but suddenly turned back at him and asked,

"Do you still miss her?"

Kaliyan keenly looked at Valli again and he recollected the birds flapping sound. Immediately he closed his ears and eyes and behaved vigorously which made Valli come and hug him and ease him. Kaliyan started to whimper on her shoulders and she hugged him a bit tighter.

"How will I stop missing her? Even the smell of your breath reminds me of her. Everything, every other thing in my life reminds me of her. I'm stuck I never moved and I still haven't got away from the flap of that bird, my bird, the longing lonely bird that waits for me…"

Valli stopped him and suddenly slapped him which made an end to his blabbering and he started crying like a child. Slowly the intensity of his crying increased and increased a lot. Suddenly Mani from the other room rushed into Kaliyan's and stood quietly,

"I think, he started listening to those flaps again," Valli told Mani.

"Let me call…" Mani was about to call the medical shop down the hill.

"No, he just needs some people around him," she stopped him and asked him to gather children for the evening to have a small feast.

She then asked him to take care of the children at their place and locked the door to give some space for Kaliyan to relax. She took the hot water and applied it to his head. She took his shirt off as well. He again got emotional and fell over her again. She tried to console him and the sunlight scorched them again through the window. She got up and pulled the curtains in and she was startled when she felt a hand on her body. She could feel him hugging her from the back. She unknowingly shed tears and remained stunned.

She turned back and wiped his tears and asked him to move away. Kaliyan moved back some steps and pulled her in. She hesitated and let him know quietly that it was time she left. Immediately he sat back at the bed and Valli walked around the bed only to get back at him from the other side of the bed and had him on her shoulders. Kaliyan started to smell her breath and inhaled inside well enough to have his desires back as much as he could. He kissed her neck and she closed her eyes slowly and her breath became heavy and irregular which got more intense. Kaliyan had enough of the delay and kissed her cheeks and slowly went near her lips and asked,

"Shall I?"

She gasped and nodded her head.

"I shall give one million kisses on the lips and what will these lips offer me?" he whispered in her ears.

"A smile" slowly she hissed back.

His emotions picked up a pace and he slowly caressed her over her waist and hugged her tight. She liked that and she couldn't control her and she kept away all the consumption of herself and kissed his lips and they both wished that kiss should last longer than eternity. Their intense and beautiful kiss slowly started to dilute the lips which needed rest and his hands took over. Both Kaliyan and Valli were enjoying the time of their lives as Valli's lips began to pain and Kaliyan's lips started to wet. She got up and sat on him and saw Kaliyan's face which was sweating and his eyes were telling what he needed. She wanted it but she couldn't say and Kaliyan needed it but he couldn't initiate it. But somehow deeper the intense became, the deeper the intercourse began. So, for the first time, Valli was feeling something like that in her life. As everything was going on higher than Twin Towers. The sunlight struck it like the aircraft that sneaked into the room as the curtain swayed away. Kaliyan noticed that someone was watching them and he rushed to the windows and opened them to see Mullan who ran away from his house backyard.

That evening, when the summer's brighter moon was about to appear, Marthandan and Mullan along with the Chithirai street young boys were having a party. They were roasting Kaliyan to their hearts' content about how he fell in that thorn massacre at the church in the evening,

When Mullan was about to say something about Kaliyan, Marthandan cursed at Kaliyan. Mullan was giggling a bit and said,

"Eda Marthanda, do you know something? Why are you worried about Kaliyan? You are great,"

"But who knows? Everyone always rates Kaliyan higher than me. Not today. Right from the day I met him, it was all about him, him, him. He studies well, he plays well, he is strongly built, he is good looking, and now he is a noble person who doesn't drink, doesn't smoke and surely he doesn't have any bad habits either. So even Isabella Ma rates him higher and that bloody father too. Sorry Praise the Lord…oh no the Lord is even bloodier."

"Eda mone, stop stop…enough of these. Listen to me carefully. We have a chance to pull down Kaliyan to nothing."

Marthandan kept his wine glass aside and eagerly listened to him.

Mullan continued, "You know the girl Valli!"

Marthandan nodded.

"She seems to be a bitch of Kaliyan, kind of filthy whore. I saw it with my eyes, you know what she did to him." By the time he told this, Marthandan gave him a tight slap which made Mullan fall down few steps from his place. He got up quickly as the boys there went silent mode and they couldn't see the reddish fiery eyes of Marthandan which they had never seen before. Mullan slowly realized how furious Marthandan was and eased him off with his words and he again pushed him back and went into the house.

Mullan saw the boys who were silently observing and he approached him inside to see Marthandan looking at the mirror. He closely looked at Marthandan and he could sense that he was doing something fishy. He was looking at him in the mirror and wiping his face with his palms and slowly his index finger to his nose. Soon, Mullan reached him stopped him, and said,

"Yeah, this is what I have been trying to tell you. These are all because of him, this is the chance to finish him off. We should do it."

Marthandan's face changed a bit and said in a husky tone,

"I can't do this to a girl who's involved, and…"

"And what? Come again?" Mullan fumed.

"He was my friend. Once he was my everything. I never lived a day without thinking about him."

"You never stopped thinking about him even today. This is why he is getting a better place than you. The emotional fool. The entire village sees you as the clown.

Even that useless Nun you are routing for, she never cared about you. Remember your age, you are going to be fifty in some years but you still think you are in twenties. Throw off your concern for him and stand with me. You are the Moothakani for our village and after that, the entire village which made fun of you and never stood for you at your tough times, will stand for you to do something…"

As Mullan was telling this, Marthandan's face again changed, and decided to go with Mullan's evil strategy.

"Let me finish him, let me finish your friend Marthanda," he furiously told him in that same doozy tone. They again started to have drinks outside. As the boys were enjoying the drink party, they were interrupted by a boy who ran in and said,

"Marthanda etta, you were called by Father to assemble at Isabella Amma's house with the scarf. Everyone."

"Why so? In this evening? Tell him Chetta is busy," Mullan told the boy.

He replied, "Okay then I'll get only Kaliyan etta there."

All of a sudden, the next second, spilling all the drinks over the place, Marthandan got ready and tapped Mullan.

"Eda Mulla, we need to go there before him. Get up I think the plan worked."

At Kaliyan's house, Valli was sitting at one corner being drained out of tears as she cried a lot that Mullan saw what has happened.

"He would have told everyone about this now," Kaliyan murmured. She looked at him and said, "I should have stayed in the Church. It's my fault."

"It's no one's fault, we did nothing wrong. I know where the fault is…and I will take care of the fault that was made."

The boy came to Kaliyan's Aavani street and called Kaliyan to come to Isabella's along with the scarves.

Chapter Twelve

As Father said, the rituals of Vadamala bootham pooja were about to be planned at Isabella's house that evening. After having a small feast at their home Kaliyan and Valli got ready to attend the meeting. They took the bike and the neighbors took their children inside their homes as if it was a sin to look at both. On their way, everyone looked at them so weirdly that made Valli felt uncomfortable and embarrassed. She started to cry and asked him to stop at the center of the village where the church and the temples of Sasthan and Vettikadu pei were. She got down from the bike and started crying in the temple as she couldn't bear the shame and the laugh of the people.

Some of the men and women looked at her like she did something that was going to cut the world into two.

"Hey…" Kaliyan shouted at Valli which made the entire place look at him. He shouted at everyone. Immediately Valli hopped on the bike and they moved to Isabella's. At some distance, they were followed by Marthandan and Mullan.

At Isabella's, Mani reached there early and made Isabella sleep. She was sleeping and it was Mellissa who arranged the chairs and water for the meeting. Father asked Melissa to stay after the meeting. Valli straight away went into the house to work in the kitchen.

Melissa looked at Valli and smiled. She hesitantly smiled back because the village members spite her.

Many of the people who turned up and waited there were giving an eye at both Kaliyan and Valli as if they were about to eat their food. Marthandan and Mullan who were in half drunken stage somehow managed to stay steady at the place.

"Village is running out of noble people," a lady from the crowd lashed at Kaliyan indirectly. Both Mullan and Marthandan giggled between themselves. Kaliyan immediately took a step forward towards Marthandan but he was instantly stopped by Father who asked him to remain silent.

Some of the main heads of the village also turned up there, including newly married Selvam's daughter Lakshmi and her husband, Mathesh. Everyone in the crowd was asked to tie up the scarf on their head. Father initiated the conversation.

"As a Christian, I should not be involved in this but as a part of our tribal community –"

Mani suddenly looked at Father and so did Marthandan and Kaliyan.

"Sorry, your tribal community, it is mandatory to get the Vadamala bootham's pooja started. That is how we can proceed to our Palli festival. Hope you are all aware of that. Due to that, the first initiative was going beyond Dravyapara to greet Vada mala bootham. For that, we need a woman, who can proceed further. We tried the same when last time Isabella Ma was not well. It was nineteen years ago, but it hasn't gone as well as we thought. We as a community, need to get rid of those bad memories and so now we need a volunteer to do that. Whoever is not willing or doesn't want their family members involved in this, you can throw in your scarves."

Instantly, Mathesh threw his scarf down as a sign of unwillingness as he didn't want his wife to get involved in this.

"Eda, Mathesh eh, why are you doing this? As part of the ritual, they had to be kept untouched by their husbands for at least seven days. Don't you know that?"

A trace of anger lingered in his eyes when he looked at his wife. Many men who were having daughters, sisters, wives, and mothers at home also threw in their scarves. Father observed everything and started to take note of the remaining women in the village,

Suddenly another scarf was thrown in the middle. Father looked at it and was confused about who else was remaining. He looked up to see that it was Kaliyan.

"Kaliyaa, you should have a woman at home to object to this. You don't have anyone," Father whispered to him.

"No father, I don't think that so. I have someone at home whom I have known since she was small. It's Valli."

The crowd started to murmur about the decision.

Valli was about to take the rice pan out of the stove but her hands stumbled and the pan hit the floor spilling rice all over the room. She couldn't believe what she had heard. Father Ben again objected him by saying that they can't practice these type of relationships inside the village. But Kaliyan was trying to convince the father that she was going to live at his home.

"Just because she studied and lived under your expenses don't mean that she could be your wife."

"There is no probability father. We are anyway going to get married after our festive season." Kaliyan loudly marked his statement in front of the village main heads.

"No, this is not the place to confess your dirty personals. Everyone knows how dirty you are Mr. Kaliyan. Now we all know what you were doing with that girl in your house. We don't allow such practice in our culture." Mullan came forward and spitted his words. Suddenly a barrel of water leaked from the house. Valli started to cry inside the house near Isabella who was in deep sleep.

When Melissa came with a towel to wipe the water, she listened to those words of thorn uttered by Mullan.

"Mellisa, you shouldn't interfere with the things going to happen outside now." Father saw Melissa coming into the crowd and stopped her.

"Listen, Melissa, you are not supposed to come here. Please stay in."

"No father. Since the entire village is shaming a girl for being a girl and all of these people including you remaining silent for all these slut shaming, I have to step out."

The crowd was looking at Melissa and she looked at both Mullan and Marthandan pulling a disgusted face.

"A crooked nun who didn't even know what is going on in her life comes out for the support of another woman who is someone's sidekick," Mullan again furiously showed his disinterest.

"Melissa, it is not about what you think. As we thought Valli may be a go to contender for the nude walk around Dravyapara as she was living her life from her childhood serving for this village. And also she doesn't have parents and no one is going to object her but all of a sudden Kaliyan is bringing up chaos," Father debated with Melissa.

"Did you say no one is going to object to her? Yes, she doesn't have anyone now, but she has herself, hasn't she? It's her body and her soul to decide everything. Not any meetings," Melissa fumed at him.

"Okay even if they are about to get married, the prescribed girl has to be untouched for at least seven days. If he's noble enough, can he confess that she is untouched for seven days and then throw down the scarf?" Mullan queried.

Father nodded at Mullan and looked at Melissa. She turned at Kaliyan and he saw her.

She went closer to Kaliyan, and Marthandan's eyelid popped out. She hesitated to talk with Kaliyan and he turned his face away from her. Slowly gaining confidence with the help of a deep breath, Melissa opened her mouth.

"It's time for you to do what you are supposed to do. I've talked to you after all these years for the sake of Valli, not for you. Please stand with that girl and do the wiser thing."

Marthandan and Mullan saw each other and landed their sight again on Melissa.

Kaliyan stepped ahead of the father and said,

"Yes we had sex in the afternoon, she cannot be prescribed for the rituals at Dravyapara."

Everyone was stunned by his statement and Mullan looked angry. Melissa turned at him as well and she couldn't stand the sight of Marthandan for what he did. He couldn't look at her either. Melissa closely looked at his face and the stare lasted for some seconds but her eyes didn't have anything soft. It was all hatred and dirt about Marthandan.

"Oh oh oh…enough of these dramas, Enda ponnu Father eh, this woman speaks all these rules and stuff here to take that girl away and this brave soldier who stood for a fellow woman, will she accept the request and do the nude walk and rituals there beyond Dravyapara?" Mullan raised a question

"I will do," Melissa immediately accepted what he said even before he completed his question

"Melissa no. You are blessed and devoted to Jesus. You cannot do that," Father stood up and fumed at her.

"Father please, from the first second I stepped out to speak for her I knew this what would happen. Please. I had devoted my life to Jesus who devoted his life for us. Wouldn't he allow me to do this for people for that pity poor girl who is receiving the shame? Let them crucify me too"

"Melissa, don't you know the risks involved in this? No one from our village went beyond Dravyapara for years. Only Isabella Ma knows what is beyond that. It would be completely dark, and even if we go by their belief, to say for real there will be Vadamala bootham at the north, and most importantly, if something happened to you or even a slight blood strain at the ritual, you would be evicted out of the community with the brand "sinner", please don't," Father again requested her.

"Father, remember when I first wore the Nun sari, you said that I was looking similar to Mother Mary, the mother of Jesus, the blessed among the woman, the chosen one… now I wish to let that come real Father."

Father couldn't answer and the crowd slowly faded and the scarves thrown were taken by them as well. Kaliyan took his scarf called Valli and hugged her. Melissa again looked at Marthandan and stared at him and went inside the house. Kaliyan slowly approached Mullan had him face to face wore the cooling glass, and said.

"Umbrella should be opened up soon at midnight, count your nights."

✳ ✳ ✳

On that day of Vadamala bootham's pooja, no house in the village should eat meat or anything that is not vegetarian. The villagers were very concerned about the holiness of the ritual.

At the Sasthan temple, in the center of the village, some of the villagers gathered to initiate some pooja for Sasthan before the ritual actually began. Father Ben who just came there was greeted by all. He initiated the pooja. He sat in a place and started reading the bible.

✳ ✳ ✳

At Marthandan's, Mullan was cooking a beef curry without masala so that the villagers wouldn't smell the meat being cooked. Marthandan was having a peg of whiskey he bought from down the hill. He also was guarding the home from not allowing anyone inside. Even if someone came near his house, he easily guided them away for any silly reason.

✳ ✳ ✳

At Isabella's Mani was working heavily alone and he was setting up the fire pot and the turmeric powder which had to be applied on the skin of Melissa when she was to do the ritual. Isabella was bedridden and was unable to even tilt her back from the bed. Mani was helping Melissa clean the house as the villagers would be served dinner there later that day. Some hours later in the day, Valli came to the house with Kaliyan. He didn't enter the house but called Mani to come out to have a conversation. He gave the bag to Mani that he left at his house which had the passport application copy.

"Eda Mani, don't be reckless. Keep it safe and secure. You don't want to miss this making the Thiruvananthapuram journey useless. You are still a kid."

"Chetta, that is not the issue. Anyhow it should be in your house and also I was about to do all these works alle? Who else is here to assist Isabella? What will she do if I'm not here? Tell me."

Kaliyan answered nothing and looked at Isabella being bedridden.

Mani got emotional after seeing her and said,

"Same like her, who else do I have if she leaves me?"

Kaliyan consoled him and hugged him to see him whimper on his shoulder.

"Let this festival happen well. We will take care of her. She is around a hundred years older than you and look how many generations she has conquered. She is the real Queen."

Inside the house, Melissa was bathing alone and she saw her breasts being untanned and her skin being so fairer than her normal tone as the life hadn't given a fair amount of chance for melanin to kill her fairness. To walk the street alone in the night, she took a bath and had to be fasting so that she would be given milk and the honey which was the Kanikar's main food that they extract. She was being locked at a room made by Mani using Coconut tree's leaves.

❈ ❈ ❈

The dusk appeared. At the center of the village, some villagers including Father Ben were asked to leave the place and go back to their houses.

At Aavani Street, Kaliyan was carrying Cinderella outside his house and was also asked to go inside. He took her inside and asked her to play with the other kids inside the room and asked everyone to stay inside until he came back. He went out and took his bike despite the warning.

❈ ❈ ❈

At Chithirai Street, Mullan and Marthandan were boozing up inside the house without the knowledge of the neighbors.

"Eda, this beef is so different without masala. It tastes even better with this whiskey," Marthandan started enjoying his drink.

* * *

Kaliyan went behind the church. There was a place where they made bio-fertilizers from the bio wastes. With the sunset, the dusk turned into darkness as it was a no-moon day. He stopped his bike and went into the darkest place without light. He slowly searched for something and finally found the hand-held thin spear. That was used for hunting from the roof of the small cottage there. He took it outside and tied it with his bike and checked around whether had he been watched or not.

* * *

At Marthandan's, when they both were enjoying their drink, they suddenly heard the door knocks. They had no idea who that was as the entire village members locked themselves inside the house ahead of the ritual. Even drunkards wouldn't roam around. They were afraid of being caught. Mullan wiped his face, hid everything with his lungi, and asked Marthandan to check. He slowly opened the door with guts to see Mathesh, the newly married guy. He immediately pulled him inside and scolded him.

"Shhhhh, eda Marthanda, I'm not here to make an issue."

Mullan giggled after hearing the word "issue".

"Tell me the reason," Marthadan fumed out of frustration.

"It has been some weeks since I got married. You know how strongly I had thrown my scarf in the meeting. That is how frustrating it is with my wife. So I'm boozing up daily but I didn't today as I'm scared that my father-in-law would find me. But I know you wouldn't spare a day without drinking. So I just turned up here. Please don't leave me, my friend." Mathesh pleaded.

Mullan asked him to sit and have a drink. Mathesh boozed himself and asked for a good side dish. They served him the beef fry.

Mathesh almost puked.

"You know what is so special about beef? It is not the flesh. It is about the masala and the fried scrambled coconut sprinkled over it. The extracted coconut oil, the garam masala, coridander masala, and the turmeric essence are what would make a beef curry special. Not this one."

"Eda Mathesh-eh you came here to drink a droplet of whiskey alle? Now you are demanding a Malabar-style beef curry aano, endha da mone idhu?"

"Hey, we all know that. But we cannot go out it is restricted," said Marthandan.

"Huh? Marthandan obeying restrictions? In which world would that happen?"

Marthandan looked at him.

"Eda Marthanda, I know a place behind my in-law's friend's house. There is turmeric land and he also cultivates some spices as well. I have seen it. We can go there, pick some and I will make this a special one. No one will see us and smell us. Even if they smell who would dare to come out and check us? The entire village is now under lockdown. We can do it," Mathesh insisted.

Mullan opened the door, adjusted his lungi, and was followed by Marthandan and Mathesh. These three roamed in the streets.

✳ ✳ ✳

At Isabella's Mani left the house after looking at Melissa. Valli applied a turmeric paste over her body as if she was going to be tandoori. Melissa wore a skinny transparent petticoat that was tied above her waist. She touched the feet of Isabella who was blabbering the same "Hare Krishna' slogans and "Bible verses" randomly. Melissa was taken out by Valli and she thanked Melissa with both her hands. Melissa smiled and said, "Let the lord be with you." The door closed, and Melissa took the flower pot consisting of honey, milk, corn, rice, and some paddy as well. She removed her petticoat and saw above the sky to see no moon. She felt a bit lonely as her only friend was also absent to see her naked. She came out of the house and started towards Dravyapara.

✳ ✳ ✳

Those three finally came to a farm where all those spices were cultivated and they were ready to take that. As it was pitch dark, they were finding it hard to find the others as well. Marthandan was struggling to pluck some turmeric at one end and Mullan was searching for something as he couldn't see anything in the dark. He finally found a hand in the dark, pulled it out and said,

"Eda Marthanda, it is so dark today." But he immediately sensed that was not Marthandan. That was Kaliyan.

Mullan ran back and hit Marthandan with fear as he could now see him from a distance with the help of Kaliyan's bike headlight where the thin spear was tied. Mathesh untied that and threw it to Kaliyan. He caught that.

"Eda Mathesh eh, you traitor," Mullan fumed at him but Marthandan closed his mouth.

Marthandan immediately saw Kaliyan approaching and he crushed the turmeric with his hand and sprayed it on his face. He started running along with Mullan. Kaliyan chased them after wiping out the turmeric powder from his face.

Mathesh started the bike but Kaliyan turned off the engine and asked him to maintain silence.

"No one should know that we are outside. That is exactly how no one would know how those men were killed."

He started chasing them and they slowly ran without any noise trying to evade the man with a spear. They ran from east and west to north and south throughout the village. Finally, Mullan and Marthandan reached the center of the village, the Sasthan temple.

Mullan bent down on his knee and pleaded to lord Sasthan to save him. They suddenly heard the chain sound that was plugged with the spear and they immediately hid from them to the side of the temple. Kaliyan with his furious face was sweating out in anger. They both heard Kaliyan's heavy breaths.

Both Mullan and Marthandan were able to see Kaliyan approaching the temple. With the darkness being surrounded, they couldn't see Kaliyan. But they heard the chain sound of the rings those were plugged with the thin spear. They both evaded brilliantly inside the temple. But Kaliyan was a step ahead of them.

He opened the tap and made the floor wet on one side and left it dry on the other. Then he made his thin spear make a sound, and then he slowly listened to some footsteps. He followed the two pair of wet footsteps and finally found them near the Vettikadu pei statue. He held the chain of the spear made it mute and aimed at Mullan. But at his stance, he slipped out of his stance and missed it which helped his hand to release the chain and make the sound. Suddenly Mullan and Marthandan realized his presence and started running out of the temple.

Kaliyan approached them ahead again and chased them to a small hundred-foot mount. Grabbed the feet of Mullan and asked, "How dare you interfere with Valli? This is your last day, mone."

Marthandan pulled him ahead and he successfully saved Mullan from him. He slipped suddenly and fell from the mount and he lost Mullan somewhere in the dark as well.

Marthandan was carried away by the slope and got bruises and his neck was also pinned by a plant. He fell finally from the mount and reached the road. He gasped and held his mouth as if he should not shout. He cried holding his mouth and screamed inside in pain.

He then suddenly listened to the sound of that chain again. His eyes lit up and he got scared. He turned away and stood to see Melissa face to face. It was the sound of Melissa's anklets.

Both were in shock and didn't utter a word.

Melissa saw him being wounded and was so curious about what must have happened. But she wouldn't want to talk to him and she didn't have any other option of saving her nudity from him.

Marthandan tried to run away from her and he heard the original sound of the spear of Kaliyan. On hearing this, Melissa understood the situation and planned something out of serious pressure.

She went near to Marthandan and grabbed his wrist after so many years and asked him to run along with her. Kaliyan came down and he could sense Marthandan running and he chased him.

Then, both Melissa and Marthandan reached the Dravyapara and Marthandan stopped. Melissa pulled him beyond the Dravyapara. Marthandan turned to Melissa to see her fully nude body in the light from the candle at the

Dravyapara. He was trying to take his eyes away and ended up crying.

"Marthanda…" Melissa called him.

Marthandan heard the words of honey, that Melissa called out to him after these many years, he turned to her without any hesitation.

"Run with me, run along with me for your life," Melissa asked him.

Marthandan nodded his head and said "I shouldn't cross Dravyapara as a male. We all know what we were told. The story of the nude goddesses, the story of Dravyapara, why it is closed. I shouldn't do the same sin again, please."

"Marthanda…I don't know what happened but I know something is seriously up with you two. He will kill you. Save your life come with me. He will not cross this. At least do this what I say…at least for now"

Marthandan looked at her eyes shedding tears and he saw her shed a drop of tear too. Then he looked at her eyes closely and she opened her heart which led her cry for Marthandan, the lost relationship of her, the lost love of her life, and the uncanny emotion of her finally broke.

The "real nudity" of her was revealed not from her body but from her heart. Her naked heart came near to Marthandan and kissed him on the lips.

After a few seconds, they both heard Kaliyan and they ran beyond Dravyapara becoming one of the very few persons after Isabella to go beyond the north of Dravyapara, where they believe Vadamala bootham lives. They were followed by Kaliyan next in chase of Marthandan.

The complete darkness helped them to avoid him again. Marthandan was too scared to open his eyes as if Vadamala bootham may catch him. He followed Melissa blindly and they hid behind a bush. She plucked a leaf from a plant. Broke its stem and applied it on the wound on the neck of Marthandan and shut his mouth with her hand. She also plucked some stems from there and crushed them and applied it on the neck of Marthandan again. He screamed silently out of pain and Melissa closely saw the stems of those plants grown there. They looked closely again and the silence composed a better music then.

Meanwhile, Kaliyan held his chain from the spear and slowly approached the place where he could hear the stems of the plants being moved. Kaliyan held his nerves and slowly approached there and he sensed the stem being plucked there.

He aimed at that hand which plucked the stem and decided to ping his spear. He took a great elevation and pinged at the shoulders of those hands.

A huge scream filled the forest beyond Dravyapara forest. Even if Vadamala bootham exited, it would've vacated the forest at that wildest scream. Kaliyan took back the spear and closed his eyes in satisfaction and wiped away the blood splash from his face.

Kaliyan took a rise and looked up the sky in satisfaction and only being shocked to see Marthandan standing in front of him at some distance. Melissa had her ears closed and stayed very close to him. Kaliyan was confused about whom he had stabbed a few seconds ago.

He moved the plants away to see a foreigner along with a lady who was not screaming but held the man being laid down with the bloodshed. It was none other than Brandon and Alyssa. Kaliyan had stabbed him.

Chapter Thirteen

At Adina's, Christopher Raj opened the house and called Evangeline to take care of their admitted son and informed her that they had reached. Adina was still nervous and anxious about meeting Alyssa and she was always scared of her father. She texted Alyssa.

"We reached home, where are you?"

She didn't get a reply and she got the anxiousness even harder.

Her father again asked about the person who helped them. Then they heard the calling bell. It was Alyssa who had come home.

Adina invited her in with an anxious face and her father gave a rave look at the girls.

"Pa, this is Alyssa, from Australia," she introduced her to her father.

"Australia? Which part of Australia? Victoria? Queensland? South or West Australian or else Tasmanian? Which part do you belong?" he asked.

"Umm, well I'm from Brisbane, a Queenslander hmm," Alyssa broke the ice within her.

"Why are you here? How do you know Adina?" he again asked her in an authoritative voice. Alyssa then gasped a bit and answered.

"Umm well, Mr. Christopher…I'm here for my girl, she is on her deathbed, and I need to treat her better. I read in my PG thesis that this part of the world contains numerous medicinal stuff to heal the disease. So we are here to take that."

"Disease? What kind of disease?"

Both Adina and Alyssa were looking at each other and she still didn't know the cause of her visit to India.

❋ ❋ ❋

The same evening, Brandon hit Joseph's place. His mother was making a coffee and Brandon couldn't resist. He went straight to the kitchen to ask and know how she was preparing the coffee.

"This is so brilliant. A genius move mate. See how thick and volumized the milk is. I hope I should taste it right from the kitchen."

"Jo…please ask your friend to be calm or else he will "face" the coffee," Jesintha ordered strictly.

"Jeez, what did I do mate?"

She served the coffee and saw Brandon with a judgmental look as his appearance seemed to be alien for her. She was so curious to know about his tattoos and their meanings.

"I have never seen such a strange friend of yours in my life. Oh lord! Why is he here?"

✽　✽　✽

At the cell in the Police station, Peter Durai was imprisoned for a night before he was produced in front of the magistrate. His henchmen surrounded the police station but Arockiyaraj threatened everyone.

"Hey where is my dinner?" asked Arockiyaraj from his seat.

Peter Durai saw him from the lock up and he was keen on initiating the conversation, but Arockiyaraj didn't bat an eye.

"This is not at all good for you. Please re-think about what you are doing. You have touched the wrong path man. I can't see myself in this lock-up for another twenty minutes," he blabbered from the cell.

Arockiyaraj didn't give heed to him and finished Parotta and mutton curry for dinner. Then he crushed the papers and threw them in the dustbin. He then opened the cell and went inside to talk with Peter Durai.

✽　✽　✽

"Erica...Erica Clarke, my girl," said Alyssa, and her eyes sparkled when she uttered the name "Erica".

"Is she your daughter?" asked Christopher with a curiosity.

"No she isn't, she is my girlfriend," she replied strongly.

"Oh, your friend?" Christopher confirmed again.

"No, she isn't, she is my girlfriend. I mean yeah, Girlfriend."

He seemed worried about facing Alyssa and looked at Adina with a disgusted face Adina didn't have any clue on how to react or how to answer her father.

"Yes, Mr.Chris. The thing is, she is on her deathbed. She is suffering from a disease. I don't want to tell you that name. It hit the most beautiful part of her body…"

"Cancer?" Adina interfered which made Christopher stare at her and he immediately asked her to step away from their house.

*　*　*

"This coffee tastes amazing," Brandon exclaimed in his own way.

"Oh Jesus Christ, how many types of people you had created?" she blabbered.

"Maybe four, no twenty? No thirty. That is why we celebrate Pride month every June since it has thirty days."

"No, no mate. She can't understand that," Joseph warned.

"It's my duty to explain to Mrs. Jesintha."

"Did you call me out by my name? You know who I am? you know about my age?" she lashed out at Brandon.

"What did I do? I just addressed you with your proper name, no nicks added, period."

"Joo, I can't understand a bit of even what your friend is talking about."

"Maa, wait let me explain it to you…Brandon and Alyssa are friends, he is a boy and she is a girl.'

"No Joseph, how can you decide my gender?" Brandon interfered.

"Shut up, I'm explaining…." Joseph lashed out and continued,

"Brandon's girlfriend is not Alyssa and Alyssa's boyfriend isn't Brandon. They both are gay and lesbian. They don't have feelings for the opposite genders."

"Jo, Is that good? They might end up as good scholars without distractions, don't you think?" Jesintha asked.

"Mom, listen. I'm explaining again. They have feelings for their same-gender people."

Jesintha was stunned and looked at Brandon sitting next to Joseph and gave a look that had millions of questions. She immediately asked him to move away with her eyes but Joseph couldn't understand the repeated signs.

But Brandon understood the thing and moved a step away and said,

"Man, she is asking to move you further away from me as I'm gay. Nice discrimination in an orthodox Christian family, holy Jesus Christ. Oh yeah here is your camera," he kept the camera on the table.

"Okay, enough. Why are they here?" Jesintha asked.

❋　❋　❋

"Dear, I'll be there within a week. Please take care of your little brother. You are now a seven-year-old princess of my clan, not a kid anymore. Please make sure that you lock your gates. Your granny is inside there, right? Please do not let the dogs inside. They should not enter our houses, take care," Arockiyaraj spoke to his daughter through the phone, took a chair, and sat behind Peter.

"What do you want to talk with me?" asked Arockiyaraj to Peter.

"Sir, you know what? People of our castes worship our women as deities and goddesses. Then how can we just parcel them away to a stranger who belongs to a lower caste? It is very simple. We can't even allow them to drink a drop of water in our houses, can we? But we are ordered by the government and some laws to make our women to marry them, pchh, who created these laws? Just because someone has written and modified it in their favor, people from low caste don't get to easily take away our pride. Our goddess from us. And the most important part of it is the lump of money they always loot from us through our girls," Peter explained his views to Arockiyaraj.

"Why are you giving the justification for your crimes? Is it good to kill a woman from your own caste? What does it make you?"

"It is not considered as killing. It is for our clan's pride. It is like removing the dirt and germs from our community. It is the cleaning process. Our goddess shouldn't be dirty. Our clan's pride lives in her vagina, the goddess's vagina."

Suddenly Arockiyaraj received a call from her daughter.

"Daddy, a dog entered our house. What should I do? It is barking."

"Throw the stone at the barking dog," said Arockiyaraj over the phone.

"Whooofffff, that is what I did," Peter exclaimed to him.

Arockiyaraj looked at his eyes closely and moved a step away. He turned back at him uttering nothing and closed the cell bars.

"Sir I know we are not the same, but our castes lie on the same level. But not those dogs. They always fall under us. Now you are arresting me for the sake of those dogs. What will you get? Someday, the same dog may enter your house as well, through your daughter, what will you do then? Will you kiss the dog or throw a stone?"

Suddenly a group of henchmen of Peter entered the station with a lawyer and granted the permission to speak with him.

✳ ✳ ✳

"Yes, she has cancer, Erica Clarke, one of the senior naturists in Brisbane, is affected by cervical cancer. A year back she was diagnosed with cancer and we started the treatment. But as we went by the treatment, she fell sick. The chemotherapy didn't work for her. It is killing the cancer cells and also her at the same time. At times she felt as if she was rotting in hell. It is the cruelest treatment ever. She can't drink water, but she lost her taste. The heat intensity in her body made her lie down on the surface of the sun. Her eyelids fell, she started to lose her hair, and her eyebrows began to lose its shape. I tell you what, her eyebrows are the best sight for humankind. It tells you a story. Her eyebrows hit her forehead now and then when she talks and nods, it will be like the endless waves hitting the sand beaches which resemble her forehead."

"Wait, I thought you are gay but you are exclaiming a girl this much poetically?" Joseph asked.

"No man. I'm gay but I can still love watching girls. They are the best creatures in the world, aren't they?" said Brandon.

"Jo…" Jesintha stopped her son and continued.

"Im sorry, I didn't know you guys had such a past back at your place. But why are you here?"

❋　❋　❋

"We will be here for only three days now. We already booked our tickets. Since she wasn't able to tolerate the chemo and stuff, she researched a rare medicine that is only available in this part of the world, so…"

"Adina, enough. I thought you are in love with someone. That is why I suspected that guy might have helped us. But we cannot take these shits inside our holy house. Please ask that woman to stay out, please…'

"Oh is it that easy? I get it now…Adina your father seems to be too 'Straight' so let me tell you about him, Mr. Chris, he is Joseph. I don't think he has a second name, he is a photographer, a nice guy…"

Adina closed her mouth with her palms and Christopher stared at both the girls.

"Chill, its very simple, I didn't even have to open up… too easy. Bye Mr. Chris take care…" and then she took her bag and hugged Adina.

"Hmm, Adina you are a gem. Take care of your love and be confident and courageous enough to be a successful woman. See you soon."

As soon as Alyssa left the house, the silence at their house prevailed for some minutes until her father broke it by moving the chair a bit, calling Adina to the prayer room,

"Come, Come to the Prayer room."

Adina hesitated, wiped her tears and slowly moved to the prayer room.

"I believe in one God, the Father, the Almighty, Maker of heaven and earth, of all the things visible and invisible. I believe in one Lord Jesus Christ, the only-begotten Son of God, born of the Father before all ages, God from God, Light from Light, and true god from true God. Begotten, not made, consubstantial with the Father. Through him, all things were made. For us and for our salvation he came down from heaven. By the power of Holy Spirit, I swear on him….repeat girl I swear on him." Christopher insisted Adina to repeat it.

"Dad, what do you want me to swear?"

"Does he belong to our caste?"

"Dad?"

"Does he belong to our caste?"

"Dad…I swear on the Son of God, made by the power of the Holy Spirit. I swear he is a Christian."

"Adina, which I had known from his name being as Joseph. Please mention his caste. Is he from our community?"

"Dad, I swear on Jesus Christ again. He is a Christian, believe me."

She couldn't control her tears and started crying.

"Adina, don't try to play fool with me. Answer me, which caste does he belong to?" he got irritated by her tears and grew furious and dragged down the candle stand making a heavy noise which made Adina stop crying and close her mouth.

✳ ✳ ✳

Peter Durai's henchmen were talking to him with the lawyer and he asked,

"Did you find out who that photographer is?" asked Peter Durai.

"Brother, I found out. He is nothing, he is from…he is from –"

"He is from?"

"He belongs to a lower caste and I guess he did this intentionally to pull us down and degrade our caste's name mainly by pulling you down."

Peter Durai started laughing and slowly the smile turned into an evil one.

"I will show him and his caste who I am."

Chapter Fourteen

"Alyssa, Alyssa, it's scorching hot my love. I can't bear this, save me, save me from hell, or leave me in hell."

Erica opened her eyes and flew to Alyssa who was waiting for her in a garden of daisy flowers. She went further closer to her and kissed her lips and went upside down and kissed her again. Like an angel, Erica swung around the garden and gave Alyssa some flowers after a span of rounds. She finally fell and Alyssa went quickly to check on her. She blinked and started crying holding her head and shouting like she was burning inside.

"Please rescue me, Please rescue me, Please rescue me…." The shouting went louder and louder and suddenly Alyssa splashed some water on her face which made her realize that it was all her illusions about her girlfriend, Erica. Alyssa was so obsessed with the need for the medicine that Erica herself discovered.

"When are we leaving Brandon?"

"In an hour or so. Why? Whom do you miss? Adina or Joseph?" Brandon asked while packing all their things.

"Both" Alyssa replied and continued, "Did you call him?"

"Who?"

"That guy we spoke about in Thirvanubram or somewhere?"

"Oh, it's Tirvandram in short. Manimaaran right? Yeah, I got him over the phone. He reached there. All we need to do is go there and collect the medicine and phew phew back to Australia. I love going back there."

Brandon exclaimed and went to the reception to check out. They were greeted by the receptionists and they set off them from the hotel.

They got the cab that was about to drop them at Trivandrum. Alyssa and Brandon embarked on the cab and it moved away. They left the town, glancing at those beautiful places of Kanyakumari.

Near the bus stand, Joseph was buying dinner for himself and his mom. He parked his bike aside and ordered four parottas and four idlis. A group of men in three bikes cornered Joseph and he didn't know who they were. One of the men hit his bike and Joseph got furious and lashed at him a few words. Immediately the war of words broke out between the gang and Joseph.

"Dare you spit out those words you little brat." Joseph was scolded by one of the men and he was cornered,

"Anna here's your parcel." Joseph was handed over the parcel and was immediately been surrounded by the same men when he tried to take his bike. They were intimidating and kept on asking his name.

Then all of a sudden, Joseph parked his bike away got on one of their bikes, and said,

"Okay, take me wherever you want. But make sure you drop me here as soon as possible. My food should be hot when I give it to my mom. You should move now, shouldn't you?"

They drove the bike and took him to the church near Anju Gramam and parked outside.

"Dude, I thought the problem was different regarding what we did in the afternoon. Didn't know this was a very random gospel problem, uff…let me sort it with the father."

Joseph went inside and the church's father was reading the bible and sitting on the chair. He was greeted by the father and he had known the father very well as his mom had been attending Sunday masses frequently.

"Praise the Lord Father. Father, I know there is an issue regarding those Australians but that doesn't do anything with our church. They will be leaving the town tonight. I guess they would've crossed the border by now."

Father interfered with him and said,

"Joseph, the issue is not about the outsiders. It is you dear. You are the son of a reputed teacher in the town. How can you do this?" He was confused by the statement and saw those men outside the church waiting for him. Then, father called.

"Christopher…"

Joseph was shocked and thrilled to see Christopher Raj along with Adina entering the scene. He pretended that he didn't know any of them but Father again stated,

"Joseph, how can you do that? We all know what was going on between you and Adina." Now Joseph realized what must have happened and he was thrilled to face what the very next second held in store for him. He was receiving calls from his mother.

He cut the call gained all the courage in the world and said,

"Yes, Father. I love her. If you think loving someone is an issue, we can't be standing in a church and talking about this."

"Hey, who are you? Where do you belong? Who permitted you to talk with my daughter?" asked Christopher.

"It is your daughter who permitted me. I was granted that years back," said Joseph. The clash outbroke between Christopher and Joseph. Christopher immediately caught the collar of Joseph and warned him to leave his daughter. Adina got frightened.

"Father told everything about you and your family and your disgusting caste."

Joseph got triggered and got rid of his hands from his shirt and adjusted his hair.

"Adina, I told you right? Even Jesus Christ won't be enough to make me holier for these craps."

"Don't act smart man. I know why you loved my daughter. You have been told right? To love her, to marry her, you would demand me for ransom money? I know everything about you and your caste men. This has become your routine right?" Christopher fumed at Joseph but only ended up making him laugh. He started to laugh uncontrollably.

"Who told you all these stories? Uncle, you are a daydreamer. You write great stories of your own and please remember, if I want to demand ransom money by marrying someone I would have loved the daughter of some millionaires not the daughter of a small-time businessman in a small town like Kanyakumari."

"Joseph please take the side of peace..." said Father.

"Did you take it, Father? Even after all these years of performing rituals and praying for an eternity in front of that crucified son of God, you still have the pride of your caste. Please don't tell your God about this," Joseph roasted.

"Joseph, you need to be clear with this. Every clan has its practices and culture. Even in the bible, we are told about that. Even Abhraham made sure his daughter married from the same caste, and they told there are so many places where castes were mentioned in the bible," Father replied.

"Yeah, they told...but where was written? Did the son of God, our messiah told us? Hmm, great father I hope you got some evidence for your point. At which place it is written that the caste which Joseph belongs to should be considered as the lower one? Did they mention that father? May I know which testament it is.? The page number of it, maybe?"

"Father, please enough of these craps. Please ensure that this beggar doesn't beg behind my daughter."

Joseph got furious but simply he simply laughed it away again.

"Uncle, you are again failing at your point. Which period are you living in? I don't need any of yours. I have everything of my own. I have my bike, I have my iPhone, and to be honest the lens of my camera is costlier than your two-wheeler. What should I need from you?"

"He came to his point, right? See father. He is showing off everything and faking himself as rich and made my daughter fall for him," said Christopher.

Immediately Joseph shouted and fumed at him.

"You don't dare to speak about my girl. She wouldn't fall those. Aren't you ashamed of shaming your own daughter? Is this why we saved your son from the case? Enough, I don't have time for these shits. I'll come to your home properly and ask for your daughter's hand for marriage. We both don't have intentions to elope away and hurt your sentiments and affection. Let Jesus decides who gets to be together," he said this and greeted Father and left the place and asked the men outside to drop him at the place he was picked up.

Suddenly a person got down from the Scorpio car. Joseph gave closer look at the person and found that to be Arockiyaraj, who was in mufti.

"Sir, glad that you are here. Happy to be meeting you." Joseph greeted him.

"Joseph, right? Seems like you are an ambitious person and a talented guy. You have a bright future. Why are you sneaking your nose into unwanted problems?"

"Sir, I did it for my girl and I had known that you were also looking for the same guy. Sir, you are one of my inspirations –."

"No Joseph, I can't be because I too have a daughter at my home. Very little one but when she grows up what will I do if someone like you tries to enter our house?"

"Sir, what are you trying to convey?" Joseph sensed that something was wrong and checked whether someone was around the place. But unfortunately, he found none other than their men and Arockiyaraj. He then saw Adina and Christopher Raj coming out of the church.

"Joseph, please sit down." Joseph denied but again Arockiyaraj insisted. He calmly sat down.

"Please Joseph, sit down on the ground."

Joseph was holding his food parcel tightly and he was held firmly by Arockiyaraj on his shoulders. Joseph panicked and was embarrassed to sit on the ground in front of so many people including Adina.

"Sir, why do I need to sit on the ground?" he asked. Arockiyaraj again asked him to sit down and he pushed him on the shoulders with full strength. He fell without balance and was made to sit down in front of so many higher-caste people. Immediately the rear door of Scorpio car opened and Peter Durai came out of it.

"Because you need to be on the ground my dear…" he said and came furious at Joseph. Arockiyaraj stopped him and said,

"You said about only warning...nothing more than that as of now."

Joseph was so surprised to see Arockiyaraj supporting Peter. This happened because Peter convinced him by inducing the caste pride of Arockiyaraj's community. Also, Arockiyaraj was made to tear off the FIR copy and allegations made against Peter. He used the influence he had in the town corresponding to the big heads of his caste.

"Please remember. We higher castes people should unite against them. Only that will stop them from not taking away our girls. We should unite against them, the lower caste dogs." Peter insisted Arockiyaraj who made up his mind to take this further against Joseph.

"Enough little boy. Please leave this and get a life somewhere else," Peter told Joseph, which made him even angrier. The ill-treatment continued and Adina couldn't see her boyfriend being treated like shit in front of so many people.

"Peter, it's up to him. It has nothing to do with my daughter. Finish him off," said Christopher.

Joseph saw him and again looked down, hesitated to face Peter. But they laughed at him by making lame jokes.

"He takes photographs, right?" Peter's henchman asked

"Yeah, aesthetic photographer. Seems like a hero...my foot. Those all were for catching girls, right bro?" Peter replied.

"Look at his T shirt, as if he was born into a Zamindar family. I remember his bike he makes loud horns, thinking like a king of the road. He even horned at our cars brothers," Henchman complained about Joseph.

"Just see those shoes, as if he is some player. Why would these boys dress up so well? Only to show off to our women, bullshit," another henchman joined. Joseph was not able to do anything and quietly listened to those and sat on the ground holding the food parcel. Suddenly Peter asked him to get up and helped him. He asked,

"Please remove your shoes. Where is your home? Near Ransom Town right? Okay, you are supposed to walk like your ancestors, without a bike and shoes…okay? Please be ready. Remove your shoes. This is not a punishment. This is just to remind you of who you are and how you guys were treated. Please make sure you walk quickly or else the food will lose its hotness, okay go…"

By the time he was told, Joseph was pushed to remove the shoes, and was asked to wait. He hesitated a bit and looked at Adina. He felt so embarrassed and he couldn't do anything about the situation.

"Joseph, your warning ends here. If I see you next time stalking behind her, it won't end up with shoes alone. Remember that and walk."

Joseph moved away and he walked from Anjugramam to Ransom town. He walked over five kilometers and his sore and numb legs didn't bother him because he was carrying a whole lot of different pain in his heart. He stopped at the statue of Dr. Ambedkar and sat near it. He massaged his foot looking at the face of the statue and said nothing.

He reached the house and his mom was shocked to see his legs and feet. She also asked about his bike but he fell on the sofa with his fully wet shirt of sweat. And he gave the parcel to his mom. After a few minutes, he told her everything that happened and she panicked as it was all about the rowdies to battle with.

"Jo…you are my only asset. Please don't be involved in anything. We don't need anything," said Jesintha applying oil to his feet, massaging it.

"Ma, they made me walk just because I belong to a so-called lower caste. So I'll make them run."

"Jo?"

Joseph called Adina who was crying in her house while her father was doing night prayer in the prayer room. She picked up the call.

"Adina, I think it's time. We both need each other and it's our call to make." Without any hesitation, she got up, packed a bag, closed the door, and immediately ran outside her house.

Her father said,

"I believed in you. I never locked the door and you betrayed me."

Adina replied, "Pa, I wasn't obeying your words all this time. I was just waiting for his word which has finally come. Let me go."

She ran away from her house, and Christopher immediately called Peter's men.

On the highway of Marthandam, near the Kerala border, both Adina and Joseph were chased by their men. They eventually took long strides and ran away from most of the men. He stopped near the checkpost and asked Adina to get down. It was almost over ten in the night. The road was alone in the light of sodium vapor lamps excluding a tea shop where only two people were present.

She took a bag and stood alone while he parked the bike. He ordered two teas, and they drank it. All those men were waiting for Joseph to return as of that late night no bikers were allowed inside Kerala without being checked or without a proper permit. So the henchmen were waiting for him to return anyhow.

They slowly saw them. A nice old Malayalam song "Nee madhu pagaro" from Moodalmanju movie was playing in the tea shop. They listened to it and checked at the highway as well.

He paid the bill and asked her to collect the balance. She grabbed her bag and they both saw a cab approaching them from the highway. It stopped. They both got in the cab and it passed the Tamil Nadu border and entered Kerala successfully. It was Alyssa and Brandon who were informed by Joseph and they acted accordingly.

Brandon asked Joseph, "Mate, shall I show my middle finger to the men you were chased by?"

"Yes, you can. But we are now far away from them. I guess they can't see you doing this," said Joseph.

"No, I know that but only doing this will make me a kickass saver of life. I have also seen people doing this when they rescue someone by car. They used to put their hands outside and show the middle finger." Brandon insisted on doing that even after they were a kilometer or two away from them.

He finally, raised his hands through the window and showed the middle finger to the empty road, the highway to Thiruvananthapuram, via Parashala.

Chapter Fifteen

They reached Thiruvananthapuram earlier and went near Vizhinjam port and decided to have midnight coffee. The time was half past two. They hit a cafe at Vizhinjam and ordered two coffees latte and a ginger tea. Adina didn't want anything.

"Joseph, please don't think about anything that happened back there. Do whatever you wish for now. You would have been killed by now. Thankfully you are alive now," Alyssa calmed him down.

"I don't understand the system. In which world someone gets killed for loving someone? I still don't get this theory," Brandon blabbered, but Joseph was thinking deeply about something and he seemed worried about it. Brandon tapped his shoulders and said,

"I know you are concerned about your mom."

"No, my mom knows to take care of her and I made a plan to safeguard her as well. But I'm worried about my bike which I left at Prashaala check post. I can't even think what would have happened to my bike," Joseph worried.

"Dear bro, I guess they must have burnt down your bike."

"What?"

"Cool. They would have burnt you instead if you had been caught by them, mind you."

"Alright, why are we here? What are we going to do?" Adina asked.

"I'll explain Adina. You know where we are now?" Alyssa asked.

"Vizhinjam Port, I guess near the shore."

"Yeah, exactly, but this place has another name, Kanthaloor Salai. It was historically driven by a famous war between Cholas and Malai-Alargal ruled by Cheras. It was the clash of the titans back in the tenth century."

"Wait, what is that to do with your medicine?" Joseph asked.

"I found this medicine because of this war. Let me tell you."

Alyssa started explaining the whole story to them. She started with the strong sea breeze of early morning near the starting point of the western coast of India.

"Erica and I were college mates in a very small town called Mackay of Queensland, Australia. We have known each other since we were sixteen. I never thought that these significant types of sexualities existed. Even I thought I was straight and she thought she was straight. She even had a boyfriend at our pre-college when we studied biotechnology. But that didn't work out for her. She was so worried and she used to dump everything on me.

We got along very well and later I found out that I may have feelings for Erica. At first, I thought that was just an infatuation. But one day when we slept over in her home, we both found out that we had feelings for each other. We started making out in her room and that eventually led to a relationship further. Soon after, we realized that we are the ones that the universe and destiny have planned to unite. But that happiness didn't last long. One day she became very tired than normal and she had been having irregular periods problem. So, we went to the medical center and they gave us the most devastating news of all time. Erica was diagnosed with cervical cancer."

"Her parents weren't supporting us and I didn't have much support from my side ever since I was a kid. So we decided to move away from Mackay to Brisbane. We found a rental house near the hospital and began the treatment. But when it started, the real trouble began too. My most beautiful babe started to lose her charm due to an unwanted character in her cervical tube. The process of chemotherapy started killing her along with the cancer cells. I was so worried to see her. One day she decided to read in her bed. She was reading everything. She read science, mathematics, and history. She loved Indian history and she came to know about the Battle of Kanthaloor Salai, which happened exactly at this very place where we are now sitting and having ginger tea and coffee."

Joseph and Adina didn't have any clue about the place and looked at each other.

Brandon asked to pass the baton to him to continue the story. Alyssa passed and Brandon continued the story.

"After a few chemotherapy sessions, she couldn't see her baby getting rotten in that way. So she started researching the medicines that can cure cancer that are available in Australia. Eventually, she found a place called "Roger's Nurseries" in Brisbane itself. We reached out there and asked about the cultivation of the Flame Lily plant especially made in Australia. I pleaded with the manager to know about its medicinal value as it may help to cure cancer since it is an alkaloid-rich plant and it may be treated specially for cervical cancer. It was notably used to reduce the labor pain. But they were so irresponsible and they were keen on exporting them to Zimbabwe. Yes, Flame Lily is the national flower of Zimbabwe but at present, they are importing from Australia due to the high demand for its medicinal value. The Zimbabweians buy that and sell that to several countries like India, Pakistan mainly for its medicinal purposes. But in India, there is a hub present, which was less concerned and unnoticed by the people of that place as well. The place's name is Amboori."

"Where is that?" Adina asked,

"It's not far away. It is in Tamil Nadu and Kerala border. It was originally located in Tamil Nadu but when the states split, the forest of Amboori drifted to Kerala along with the village."

"But how do you guys even know about that forest? We hardly know about that."

"The history," Alyssa said and continued.

"Yeah, I said about a war, right? It tells you the story. A guy from the village itself will explain to you," Alyssa said and asked Brandon to call Mani.

By that time, Joseph received a call from his mom as she was house arrested by Peter and his men.

"Ma, don't worry please open the back door. You will see the light of the prophet there. He will take you to the safe house."

Jesintha curiously opened to see Joseph's friend Zayan sleeping with his lungi covered around his neck with his kept open.

"Joseph, the prophet is sleeping…"

"Ma wake him up, he is the guiding light, Zayan." Jesintha shook him and he instantly woke up and asked her to get on the bike. She then locked her house and took the backseat, but half asleep Zayan drove the bike to the front gate where Peter's men and the church people were furiously waiting. He then realized and swirled the bike around and rode faster. They were chased by the men and he managed to enter his street crossing Jumma Masjid near Railway station.

The men who were chasing them were surprised to see the massive crowd around the Masjid that too half past three in the morning. It was for Sahar morning during the Ramzan month. Zayan disappeared in the crowd and the men chased into the street. Peter called through the phone.

"What happened? Did you get her?"

"No Anna, she mingled with the Muslim crowd near Jumma Masjid."

"Fuck, go and get her…"

They decided to search for Jesintha and entered the crowd but they were eventually given a plate of Biriyani with curd rice and tandoori chicken. All they could see were the women with fardha fully covered and they felt that they were never going to get the lady they wanted.

Jesintha called Joseph from Zayan's house and let him know that she was safe.

Peter again called one of his henchmen and asked him to find him soon, and asked him to check every woman with fardha. Suddenly he pulled a woman and opened the fardha in the crowd. The young girl was frightened and started crying. Immediately, the crowd over there turned their heads at the men and the eventual event happened.

At Vizhinjam, Alyssa, Brandon, Adina, and Joseph were waiting for Manimaaran alais Mani, the man from Amboori. He came to the passport office leaving Isabella alone with Melissa and Valli and arrived exactly to the promised place. They accompanied him to the car and they went to Balaramapuram. They checked in at a cottage for tourists. They were relaxing in the living room and Mani looked at both Joseph and Adina and smiled at them.

"You guys eloped?" Mani asked.

"Yet to," Joseph answered.

The sun rose, but unlike Kanyakumari, it can't be seen vividly in the ocean. All were having breakfast and Joseph asked how they got to know each other.

"I told you right? The history and the evidence. It was all written by him in the WordPress blog," said Alyssa.

"What is that history? Can you elaborate?" asked Joseph.

"Our village is divided into two. A place with dense forest beyond a rock called Dravyapara and the rest is the village. We live at the rest of the place but we are not allowed to go beyond the Dravyapara. It was mythically believed that some ghosts named Vettikadu Pei, Vadamala bootham existed there. And also we are told only the virgin girls were allowed and we were not supposed to go there. It was said all mythically like as if a nude woman was saving our entire tribe and one day a rule was breached because a man saw her nude. So the goddess cursed our village. To lift the curse, we need to sow and reap within a day. Phew. It was all drama but what I found was the most prestigious medicine. Flame Lily plants are exotically grown and it can be exported for the benefit of our people. But it never happened."

"Men of all periods seem to be the same," Alyssa whispered.

"How especially Amboori got this much enormous amount of Flame lily?" Adina again curiously asked.

"The Battle of Kanthaloor Saalai. This place was called Kanthaloor before. It was named after Flame Lily. In Tamil, the Flame Lily is called "Kanthal". It was grown by people who lived here. The Cheras ruled the place. The Malai-Alargal lived here and they cultivated it. In the year 988 AD, four years after reigning as the King of Thanjavur, Raja Raja Chola decided to attack Kanthaloor with his son Rajendra Chola. It was for so many reasons and some say it was to capture the naval base of Cheras and some conspiracy theories say it was all for his brother Aditha Karikalan."

"Ehnnn?" Joseph reacted.

"Yes, it wasn't like as we read or saw in Ponniyin Selvan. Udaiyaloor Culvert says that he deported the killers of his brother. But seemed like the real conspiracy started there. He wasn't happy with the practice of not killing the Brahmins even though they committed the crime. He waited for his Uncle Uthama Chola's reign end and as soon he was crowned as the King, he chased the men whom he deported. Some say he found that they were practicing the war nuances under Namboodaris since they were Brahmins. At this very place, they were performing very unethical war practice which is using the poison of Flame Lily in the spear to kill the opponents. Somehow Raja Raja Chola came to know this and during the battle, he destroyed the Namboodari's saalai, the school where they trained Brahmins, and also destroyed and abandoned the Flame Lily Forest as no one should fight unethically using the poison. That is the same forest where we live now and in fact, that happened to be the very first military victory of Rajendra Chola in history."

"That is one such story for a very tiny flower. I hope this conspiracy stays a conspiracy or else this would have erupted some historical changes. Now I get why it is fixed as Tamil Nadu's state flower," Brandon expressed his views.

"Okay, but as you say, no one is allowed to that part of the village, that is the forest, how can you take us there?" asked Alyssa.

"That's what I need to tell you. It's been over nineteen years since the last time we had a Sasthan festival at our village along with the church festival too. As part of the ritual, our village's head Moothakani, the old lady Isabella will go nude and cross the Dravyapara and do rituals for our saviors, Vettikaadu Pei and Vadamala bootham."

Adina's eyes lit up to hear those names.

"At that time, no one in the village would be coming out. We can sneak into the place at that time and take the seeds. More importantly, we need to take the stem. It is more vital, and it needs to be processed to get rid of the poison. It's all up to you two guys now. The world needs to know about the significant element of Amboori. If it comes out, our place would be the most precious on earth, and it should be declared as the piece or part of the Sanjeev mountain that Lord Hanuman took over to Srilanka…"

All remained silent as the noon passed by. Alyssa and Brandon decided to leave Thiruvananthapuram and made sure Joseph and Adina got married there. But at the last moment, Joseph insisted on taking them along to Amboori. Alyssa first hesitated and then said,

"So, you are saying you made up your mind to join the adventure?"

"Huh, our life awaits more adventure I guess," said Joseph.

They joined them and the cab led the way to Amboori. On their way, both Joseph and Alyssa saw the sunset and smiled at each other.

"Remember?" Joseph asked.

"To see all sunsets with you?" Adina replied.

She smiled at Alyssa and asked a doubt.

"As you said about Erica, was she straight back then?"

"Yes"

"What about that boyfriend Erica had? How did he move on?"

"I don't know but later he realized that he is gay."

"Oh, where is he now? What is he doing now?"

Alyssa turned back to see Brandon listening to nice music with his air pods on.

Adina turned back and was followed by Joseph as well.

Without having any idea of their looks, Brandon smiled innocently.

Chapter Sixteen

After reaching Amboori, Mani made them stay in his house and asked Brandon and Alyssa to visit the honey-extracting farms as general foreign tourists. He went back to Kaliyan's home and he planned the things. Later, he asked Brandon and Alyssa to be ready for the project. That evening along with all the chaos, led to Brandon getting stabbed.

In the forest, Melissa was sitting behind a tree. All the others including Kaliyan Marthandan, Brandon, and Alyssa sat near. Kaliyan saw Brandon bleeding and he saw Melissa's legs. Alyssa started to cry for help. Melissa who was nude, hiding behind a tree closed her eyes tightly as she needed to treat him. Unfortunately, she was nude. The sky was even darker than the minds of people. Alyssa at one stage started crying out loud and Kaliyan shut her mouth so as not to shout. Marthandan took Brandon to Melissa and said,

"It's no matter whether you are nude or dressed up. You are going to be his goddess tonight. Come out and save him. Please behave like a human. Don't make the exact mistake our God did. Come out, nothing you do could be holier than saving him. Come and save him."

Melissa opened her eyes and came out. Kaliyan turned away, and Alyssa gave her the stems of Flame Lily they just plucked.

She applied the stem water to the wound and asked everyone to take him to the house.

"How did you get here? Who told you about this place?" asked Kaliyan.

"Mani…" replied Alyssa.

Both Marthandan and Kaliyan took Brandon to the village. They got out of the forest and stopped at Dravyapara. Kaliyan asked Melissa.

"Do you need my shirt?"

"Why?" asked Melissa.

"We are heading into the village."

"No one will be outside, and you guys have seen me fully. What to hide more?"

Kaliyan didn't reply and they took Brandon to Mani's place who was in half fainted mode.

Marthandan tapped the door. He slowly opened thinking that it must be Alyssa and Brandon.

As soon as Mani opened the house, Marthandan kicked on his chests and Joseph and Adina came outside of the room.

Adina was shocked to see Brandon's hand bleeding and Alyssa started to gasp.

Joseph panicked, and Marthandan asked.

"Eda, who are you guys? What is even happening in my village?"

Melissa entered and pulled down a lungi from Mani's tiny wardrobe and covered her shoulders.

"It's so cold."

Both Mani and Melissa gave first aid to Brandon and confirmed that it was not serious and nothing to worry about since the spear didn't travel deep enough.

"Maybe the stabber didn't have any strength," said Melissa.

Kaliyan checked whether Marthandan was laughing or not. But he didn't, instead he said,

"Melissa, please do the aid."

Kaliyan got up and decided to leave the house.

"Where are you going? It's almost sunrise. If they find you out now roaming, then all your Moothakani dreams would be in the tunnel. Stay here until I finish the ritual at the Dravyapara."

"Are you going again there?" asked Marthandan.

"I started it. I will finish it." Melissa left the house and removed the cloth over her upper body and started to walk back to Dravyapara. She took that light back from the rock. She saw into the tunnel and she could find only darkness. Not any women or any ghosts. She returned to Isabella's and knocked on the door.

Valli opened her eyes and she immediately came to open the door to see Melissa and hugged her.

Father and the other village men were informed of the successful completion of the ritual through a sound that was made built at the center of the village to make such announcements. At Isabella's Melissa was terribly sleepy as she had seen so much within a night. She was taken care of by Valli and it was almost eight in the morning. She was woken up by Valli.

Melissa wore the sari for the first time since last night. It seems more uncomfortable for her after being nude for a whole night. She missed seeing her beauty in front of the mirror. She went to Isabella who was still sleeping and almost lost in dreams with her favorites. Melissa whispered in her ears,

"Maa, I felt complete. I walked nude for a whole night, I kissed a man whom I was about to give my first kiss when I was a teen. I made him see me fully nude. Do I look like a bitch now? Not for showing my body to other men, but for kissing the man I hated for so many years for a strong reason. Also after being a nun for these many years, will the holy son of God forgive me?"

Isabella was sleeping unmoved. Melissa checked her again and she panicked and called Valli immediately. She panicked too after seeing Isabella who didn't show any signs of movements. For a few seconds they saw each other and they were about to cry. Isabella coughed and made a cross in sleep and blabbered.

"Krishnaa..." and yawned.

They both got relieved and took her and refreshed her for another day in her one hundred and seventeen-year-old life. They heard people approaching her house.

At Mani's, he had told everything that happened at Kanyakumari for Joseph and Adina.

"Do Christians have castes?" asked Marthandan.

"No, but most of our people are converted from Hinduism to Christianity but they didn't take anything. Even names were changed but they proudly kept their surnames behind it," Joseph answered.

"How does that make them a true Christian?" Mani asked.

"It takes courage to ask this. Many of our people are still living as Hindus who believe in Jesus. I never know when did Jesus believed in castes though," Adina told in a husky voice.

"They always come to a point about Abraham who made his daughter marry from the same caste and the Samarian girl story. But they won't have an answer for Jesus's caste. By the bible, if we all are created by god at the same level, how can the Lord create us with some dirt in us? Funny Christianity," Joseph told to Mani.

Marthandan said, "But we do practice a very different religion here. The type of religions we follow are nature, tribe, and the love of Jesus. And now we are going to have our festival this summer after nineteen years. No trouble should come from the outsiders. There shouldn't be any issue now. We shouldn't allow that Mani."

"I know but remember, their problem is not an easy one to solve. It needed some bold decisions to solve and they believed us. They are here for shelter. How can we just avoid them for the sake of us? Is this what Kanikar does? I have never heard of that," Mani expressed his opinion.

Kaliyan heard the sound of the announcement from the center of the village and he decided to leave the house. Marthandan who was in his half sleep, managed to wake up and saw Kaliyan.

"Eda Kaliya…shall we move?" asked Marthandan.

Kaliyan stopped a bit and was confused about what he just heard. But soon after, Marthandan realized himself and wiped his face, and stood up.

Kaliyan reacted in such a way that he pretended he didn't hear anything and left the house. Marthandan saw the couple Joseph and Adina and he uttered nothing and left the house as well.

Brandon was in deep sleep. Alyssa was washing her face in the backyard.

At Isabella, the post-ritual meeting was held. Everyone including Father and Isabella turned up alongside Kaliyan and Marthandan.

"We had fed Sasthan with satisfaction and I hope, one day, Melissa will take charge of the duty completely like Isabella ma. I'm not forcing anyone but to fulfill our needs and the purity, I suggest Melissa take over. But as Isabella Ma wishes, we need a Moothakani to represent our tribe. It is our tradition to have one. We already have two men who are in charge to lead. But who is the one, is the question. For that we need Isabella to tell…"

Kaliyan and Marthandan looked at Isabella closely and waited eagerly to listen to what she was about to tell.

"Honey…" said Isabella.

The crowd went murmuring. They started to discuss what the meaning of that was.

"We all remember what our traditional job is? We are all Kanikars, right? We used to hunt honey from bees, from the forest…don't we know?"

The crowd again murmured, but Isabella continued.

"As part of rituals before the Palli festival for Lord Jesus Christ, we should wait for our Moothakani to present the real wild honey from our very own forest for the church. Whoever gives more honey has all the rights to be claimed as the Moothakani."

Father Ben started, "Ma, we already have had enough of the delay for the Palli festival. If we didn't make this happen we would lose all the concern by the district bishop regarding our tribe's church."

"Yes, I know that…but shouldn't we wait for that? People have honey for fun but having honey isn't real fun either. Only a Kani can bring out the wild honey in its natural form. We have seen our ancestors doing that with the courage and will. Why can't these men do that?" Isabella added.

Father Ben thought a bit and asked for the consent of Kaliyan and Marthandan.

"Father, I don't think this would be good…" Marthandan hesitated.

"Father I accept the challenge, I will make this done," Kaliyan started strongly.

Valli was shocked to see him accept as it wasn't as easy as they thought.

Suddenly Marthandan who was concerned about it literally, announced;

"Father I'm going…I'll bring up the honey." Again the same crowd murmured and Father added.

"Okay, it is fixed. We will have a Moothakani even before the Palli festival. And they will deliver the pure wild honey of Kanikar to the church."

Chapter Seventeen

Cape Comorin had got no chills. Peter Durai and their men were so furious at the couple especially Joseph who did all those gimmicks alongside those Australians. He discussed assassinating both of them with the cop Arockiyaraj who then joined hands with him.

Abraham got discharged and came back home to learn about Adina's issue. He was informed about everything by his father. Their home slipped into a deafening silence as if someone could misread the house to be a library. His father had no one to scold and Evangeline Mary had no one to take care of their culinary skills. Meanwhile, Abraham didn't comment on his sister's elope but waited for his father to talk about it.

"What should we do?" asked Christopher.

"What do you think, we should do?" asked Abraham. Suddenly, they heard a car stopping at their door. It was Peter Durai with his henchmen.

"Do you think, our community deserves this? That too from your family? Imagine, Christopher Raj's daughter eloped with a lower caste boy and fell for his drama?" Peter manipulated Christopher.

Abraham lost his cool and said,

"Please…this is our family's internal affair. I wish you stay away from this and better not talk about this."

Peter giggled and said, "Hey look at this stoner, speaking facts…what's wrong Christopher? Didn't you bring up your son telling the pride of our caste?"

Evangeline Mary and Christopher looked at each other and he said,

"Peter, what happened is happened. Tell me what we need to do?"

Abraham interrupted, "Dad, why are asking that to him?" But his father stopped him and continued with Peter.

Peter looked at his face and said,

"Let me take them back to our place. You must have known where they are. Where they would have headed along with those Australian bitches in Kerala?"

"I'm not sure but she told me that she would get some medicines from a village nearby. But I can swear that had I known the place that would be the first thing I would tell you."

"Taking them is your way. Taking them away is my way. Have a good picture of your daughter. You won't see her alive again."

This statement from Peter shook the entire family. Evangeline ran to the prayer room and she started crying in front of him. Christopher was standing still, stunned.

Abraham was fuming at himself and his father and Peter eventually left the house. Abraham continued to thrash his father with words and he replied,

"Abraham, your sister was already dead when she stepped out of my house. So he's not going to do anything newer..."

❋ ❋ ❋

The village of Amboori was all set for the Palli festival. The church was decorated by the churchmen. At Mani's, all four from Kanyakumari were together. Alyssa was trying hard to connect her internet which was lower than the sea level. Mani was preparing himself to inform about those four outsiders in his house. He decided to confess it to Father so he was getting ready to go to church. Brandon was still suffering from the wound, and he couldn't walk. He was advised to rest for at least five days and they had to cancel their flights and a VISA extension should be made for which Alyssa was struggling to get her internet connected.

Adina's mood wasn't that good and so did Joseph's. They were asked to get married but they were hesitant for some reason.

"Do you think your Father will accept you both even after knowing his caste?" Mani asked Adina about it. She didn't reply as she didn't know about the hypothesis of being accepted by her father. Meanwhile, Alyssa joined the conversation.

"Mani, in only this part of the world, a Christian girl is unable to marry another Christian boy. Back in our country, Christianity forced us to get married and do stuff that we hate to do..."

Joseph who was lying down joined in.

"India is unlike the rest of the world always. It always amazes you in all aspects, whether good or bad, Christians here carried with them the caste from Hinduism, and you could see many Hindu castes in Christianity. When people converted from Hinduism, they changed their names, example Arul turned into Arnold, Sivan turned into Samuel, Lakshmi turned into Laicy, Rukmani turned into Ruth, Mariyamma turned into Mary, and Manikanndan turned into Mathew. However, the likes of the community didn't go off from them. The so-called higher caste Hindus carried that pride with them. They didn't want to leave their caste pride behind. Even though they started worshiping Jesus, they couldn't let go of their castes and those who belonged to the upper caste wanted to hold their superior position in the society. They didn't want to see the people of lower caste rise above them or enjoy an equal position with them. They wanted them to remain low. They didn't know to realize that Christianity has nothing to do with it. They were converted into Christians leaving Jesus behind and hugging Lord Krishna with them."

"Just like our Isabella Ma," Mani whispered to himself.

"Wait a minute. So are you making a statement that Hinduism is the mistake behind the caste thing in Christianity?" Alyssa asked.

"Nope, it's all about the humans. If they wanted their caste pride, they should have stuck with Hinduism itself. Who called them here?"

"Missionaries," Brandon murmured in his half-sleep.

"I wish that guy should have stabbed him in the mouth instead," Alyssa added which broke out the silence of Adina and she smiled. Joseph saw her eyes and passed the confidence and courage of existing to her. The morning dawn spread all over and Mani took Joseph and Adina to the church. Melissa saw them and felt curious about them. Mani explained the whole thing that happened in Kanyakumari and the difficulties they faced in getting married.

"My lord, I pity them. It is hard to see my children suffering in the name of untouchability. This shouldn't be the case," Father Ben uttered the words of justice.

"Father, I don't think we are getting married here. All I have in my life is my mom and now Adina, and for her, her family meant everything. Her father constructed it on his own. I can sense how long a man can stretch himself to build a family and how hard it is to have brought up a girl. We need their acceptance too. Now they are not in the right hands. I don't know what brings peace in us…" Joseph told Father.

Mani also confessed that there were two more foreigners present and they had to take a rest for some reason. He didn't tell about the flame lily from Dravyapara as it would create some unwanted Chaos.

"Lots have happened in a few days Mani. You should have taken them here instead of hiding in your place. Does Kaliyan know this?"

Mani was anxious to hide the truth but he had to. So he uncovered the whole thing and managed to get permission for them to stay in the village until the Palli festival.

"So, we have our first pair of guests for our festival, all? God bless you both. Let peace be with you both," Father smiled and greeted.

A day passed in introducing Joseph and Adina to Valli and some other villagers by Mani. Meanwhile, Marthandan went to Mani's house and found Alyssa researching the flowers, leaves, and stem of Flame Lily that she plucked the previous night.

Marthandan who didn't know to speak with a foreigner moved away. But he was stopped by Alyssa and she greeted him. He was a bit hesitant and was blushing to talk with a foreign woman. Somehow Alyssa managed to pull Marthandan in and made him sit.

"The guy who was about to be stabbed? Sorry bro, I got it by mistake. Hope you take back yours soon," Brandon teased him but without understanding the language, Marthandan delivered his trademark innocent smile as he thought he was being greeted by Brandon. He shook hands with Brandon and he felt comfortable talking with a man rather than a woman.

"Oh, you guys are sharing a great rapport in a matter of minutes though."

Alyssa wondered and Joseph entered the house and greeted Marthandan and saw him and Brandon smiling at each other.

"Oh Chetta, so good to see you...finally, you found a person right?"

"Yeah, it was very odd to stay and talk alone with a woman. I have never been with them. This white guy saved me until you came. I hope Mani should come soon..." Marthandan replied.

"Chetta, what did you find odd about this woman?"

"A woman. That is oddest of all the odds."

"Why?"

"I don't know. Hey, you guys have come from the town and must have seen so many women and their friendships but here we only see a woman as a person to marry. If not, they are our mothers and sisters."

"Oh, chetta, really? So then in this case, you cannot marry this woman, you can only marry the man behind you."

Marthandan was confused and saw Brandon closely and also saw Alyssa.

"Eda...what are you blabbering? How can I marry him?"

"That is what nature did to him. He is only into men, not women," said Joseph.

Marthandan slowly realized the scenario and his eyes went swirling inside he slowly took off his hand from Brandon and moved a bit further. He stood up from his seat and saw Brandon to his left Alyssa to his right and Joseph, straight to him.

He had no clue how to react but he was embarrassed by the situation and he kept moving away from the house. He was called by all three but he got rid of that house and came out to see Adina come in with the milk cane.

Marthandan saw her closely didn't say a word and went away.

In the evening, almost at dusk, the head men gathered at Isabella's along with Father Ben for the competition to get more honey between Kaliyan and Marthandan. They wore the traditional Kani dress with a white cloth around their waist and cross cloth across their upper body and a unique hat-like head cover.

By their tradition, whenever a man goes to the jungle for wild honey extraction, a woman from their home has to fast and light up a lamp and make sure the candle glows bright until he comes back marking the safety of the men entering the jungle. For Kaliyan, Valli was fasting and lit up the lamp, but for Marthandan he had no one at his home to do. He saw Melissa and she didn't react to him. Though she had concerns for him she didn't show them and continued to do her work as devoted to the church.

When they were ready to enter the jungle of Vazhichal, which was to the north of the Kani village of Amboori near the Tamil Nadu border, they had to cross the border to extract the wild honey. They were cheered by the people but Isabella suddenly raised her hand slowly and everyone went silent and waited for her.

"It is our tradition to extract wild honey from the jungle of Vazhichal. But back in our times, the borders were not made and we don't know about the reserve forests. But now they have to do it. It is one of the toughest jobs for them to get rid of Elephants and Tigers inside. It doesn't feel auspicious for me to send a duo of men to compete. Number two isn't auspicious. So please someone volunteer themselves to go in as the third, as three is an odd number and we always felt three as auspicious…who is in?"

A few from the crowd started murmuring it as dumbness but the majority of them remained silent. Kaliyan looked at Mathesh and waved.

"Why it is always me? I'm yet to live my life. Enough."

Marthandan looked at Maadan and he intentionally looked up at the sky and pretended that he didn't know Marthandan was calling him.

Isabella wasn't happy with the backpedaling by the people and she pointed out a person from the crowd.

"The outsider, the man who came with a girl. He has to join them. Let her girl fast and light up the lamp." It was Joseph whom she mentioned. Adina was shocked to hear this and so was Joseph. They immediately looked at each other and Joseph saw Father Ben.

"Ma, he isn't from our tribe, and he's from a caste which is considered…." Isabella stopped him before Father denoted him as lower caste.

"Do we follow that? It is almost time for Moothakani, but three is three…do the thing," Isabella ordered Father.

Father told Joseph, "There is no option to deny Isabella ma here. I don't know what she is thinking now, but you can't deny this…"

Joseph looked at Adina and she was panicking along with Alyssa. But Marthandan saw him, came to him, and said,

"Come and have fun, I will take care of you…I hope you're only marrying her."

Joseph smiled at Marthandan and he tapped on his shoulders as a sign of boosting him for the competition to accompany them.

Chapter Eighteen

The Vazhichal forest welcomed them with deep silence and darkness which was enough to add to an eerie mentality. Joseph, who hadn't been to such places before was feeling the nerve. He was accompanied by Marthandan. Kaliyan who was traveling with them took a different path and parted his way from them.

"He is dumb," Marthandan whispered and took Joseph further inside the forest. Joseph had been asking so many stories about the forest and Marthandan walked him through everything special about the place.

"Etta, do you know what the Australians are looking for?" Joseph asked.

"No, but have been thinking of helping them," he replied.

"You guys are losing out on something priceless. It is Flame Lily flowers behind Dravyapara. You guys are wasting out of a patent from it."

"What would you do with that?"

"They came here to get those."

"Why?" Marthandan curiously asked.

"To treat the cancer of Alyssa's girlfriend. It is hard for her to undergo all those, so Alyssa is determined to find a new medicine from Flame Lily, to help her and cure several cancer patients."

Marthandan stopped and looked at Joseph and smiled.

"Eda…are you a fool or what? Who told them these flowers give you that?"

Joseph was confused and wasn't able to understand Marthandan. He followed him. Marthandan stopped at a place plucked some leaves from a plant and gave it to Joseph.

"You know what it is? It is called Arogya pacha. The plant is called a Miracle Plant. The real extract of Agastya hills, where both medicine and Malayalam language were born as per the belief. It is the most powerful anti-biotic, anti-tumoral, and whatever harm humans will receive. It was a gift from our God. To be honest only a Plathi like me knows it from Kani…"

"What do you mean?"

"Yeah, I'm the Plathi of the village. In our tribe, some crucial medicinal tactics and information are passed on from generation to generation. Just like a Moothakani, Plathi is also a post that will be respected by our community. My ancestors and my previous generation passed on to my father, my father told me about the leaves."

"What about your parents then?"

"I lost them in this forest. I don't know what happened. Only the darkness of this forest has to tell." His face went down and he lost his charm completely. Joseph cheered him and asked about the medicine.

"Eda Joseph, are you a fool? You could have said them, right? It is not only about a Flame Lily. Everything written in history isn't completely true. Some are made up according to their belief. Only people and people's knowledge is true. Only a Kani knows about it, and especially the medicinal values, only a Plathi knows about it…"

Suddenly without hesitating, Joseph asked, "Etta why didn't you become a Plathi then?"

Again Marthandan looked down the sand and rocks and looked around the forest. His pupils went up and suddenly a snake went into his nose and came out of his eyes. He immediately wiped it around and reacted vigorously. Joseph wasn't sure about what was going on with him. He suddenly hugged him and had him on his shoulders. His condition seemed to get worse and all Joseph could think was to shout for help hoping to knock on the ears of Kaliyan.

Marthandan fainted and fell and was beaten by heavy fits. In the deep forest, Joseph was shouting and all he could hear back was his echo.

Kaliyan, somewhere in the opposite direction of the forest climbing the tree to extract the wild honey, heard the leaves and a slight echo of Joseph's voice. First, he ignored for he thought as he was hallucinating. But as the intensity of the voice increased he dragged himself down from the tree and followed the echo.

Marthandan was severely groaning in pain and he was thrashing his hands and legs. Joseph decided to lift him, but he couldn't do it. He tried again to carry him on the shoulders but he couldn't again. Suddenly, Kaliyan came in wiping away the trees to get some dusky light. He immediately lifted Marthandan on his shoulders and ran towards the village.

On their way, Marthandan slightly opened his eyes to see Kaliyan carrying him on his shoulders. He got him back to Isabella's and made him lie down on the floor. He was immediately treated by the people and he saw Valli's lamp and Adina's lamp glowing heavily. But there was no one to light a lamp for Marthandan. Kaliyan started thinking that not lighting a lamp would have made him go down and something must have happened. He asked Joseph and he explained exactly what he saw and Kaliyan came to the conclusion that Marthandan was facing a heavy trauma.

Then, Melissa ran into the crowd and saw Marthandan being treated. Kaliyan saw her eyes being shedding tears and he turned away pretending that he didn't see. She saw Joseph's hands that carried the Arogya pacha leaves.

"How did you get this?" Melissa asked. Joseph explained about it and she immediately grabbed them from his hands and she went inside Isabella's and washed the leaves. Took a pinch of cumin and a piece of coconut strip. She boiled them in water extracted them and asked the people who were treating Marthandan to give them to him. Melissa was acting completely different and she immediately ran into the house again, took a lamp, washed it, and lit that up. Simultaneously Marthandan was given that extract Melissa gave and he slowly opened his eyes, gaining consciousness. Melissa heard the cheer of relief outside and her lamp then glowed brightly towards her face. He slowly recovered and he was taken back to his home by Mani.

She saw him from the window and she looked at those Arogyapacha leaves in her hand.

At Marthandan's, he had been laid down and given the medicine. Kaliyan was waiting outside the house. He couldn't enter it after hating the place for so many long years. He was called by Mani and he was hesitating to go in. Meanwhile, Valli came and she asked him to go in and see his old friend. Even after Valli's words, Kaliyan wasn't able to enter Marthandan's house as he was reminded of the last day he spent in his house.

Valli held his hands and took him inside. Kaliyan saw Marthandan in half asleep and was feeling dizzy. He was surrounded by Joseph, Adina, Mani, Valli, and Kaliyan who just come in. Suddenly a sound of feet arose heavily. It was Mullan at the door who rushed in with some injuries in his neck and hand. He was shocked to see Kaliyan inside the house.

"Edo, Marthanda..." Mullan called him politely.

"Chetta, where did you go? What happened to you?" asked Mani. Mullan saw Kaliyan and both didn't react anything.

"I'm a man who can survive at any place," Mullan said and he went inside to his room.

Marthandan's eyes were half opened and he couldn't completely see the people around him, but he managed to recognize them. He saw Kaliyan's shadow and he could sense that he was around there for a while. Marthandan's breath was heavily boosting and he was getting so emotional on seeing his old friend coming back to see him without the grudge or ego or the hatred.

Kaliyan came in closer and their eyes met for the first time in so many long years. Kaliyan sat at the cot beside him and he saw his eyes tearing in joy and relief. Kaliyan stared at him and asked,

"What happened that night?"

And this happened to be the first word that he spoke to him since that night. Marthandan blinked and wiped his tears and closed his eyes.

"I know, you know something. Something has been happening with you since that night. I have never seen you trapped in a trauma. Now you entered the forest again and something disturbed you. what happened that night?" Kaliyan didn't seem to let go of what he let go nineteen years back.

Mullan from inside, coughed and Kaliyan thought that they were hiding something. He then stood up and decided to leave the house. He was suddenly stopped by Marthandan calling out his name

Mani stopped and dragged him in and Valli went to Marthandan and said,

"Chetta, please confess. Whatever it may be, please let us know. He has come back here for you, and you are everything he thinks about. Your friend has come to you, please."

Marthandan was unmoved in his bed and saw Valli. He slowly stood up and opened the door to see Mullan having a peg of drink.

He slowly moved towards Kaliyan, they were about to speak. Suddenly they heard another footsteps approaching. It was Melissa. She came out finally to check on Marthandan.

Marthandan changed his radar towards Melissa and got so emotional on seeing her turn up to see him. She came closer to him and didn't speak but gave the Arogyapacha leaves to him and saw Mani and told him about its medicinal values.

Kaliyan was still waiting to hear from Marthandan but he was stubborn not to open up about that night. Melissa didn't speak to anyone as usual and was about to leave the house. Immediately Kaliyan stopped her and finally spoke to her.

"Is this how you wanted to live? We have known each other since we have known the world. It didn't last long. Everyone is now shattered in various directions despite being in the same village for all these years. I lost Ponni at the cliff, I lost you at the church, and…I lost myself by losing him. I hope he remembers what he had mentioned when we were about to take this Kani tribe to the next level. What has happened? Has it changed? Everyone knows he is a Plathi and he knows about the medicinal values more than anyone but what has he done? All he has ever done these years is to booze up all day and all night with Mullan and dragging every issue in the village and poking at me for no reason. All because of the Ego, that I would become the Moothakani, my foot! Who needs that? Am I the one who claimed it? Melissa, you know everything about this village and you know about every person in this village more than anyone does. Tell me who claimed me as "Moothakani" back then? It is him. It is him. But now he is against it. If you want to do for your people, community, your tribe you have to be more dedicated, knowledgeable, and responsible. It is not the chieftain post that makes you a leader, it is your will and wish for the good deeds that make you a good leader."

"Edaaa….enough," Marthandan shouted at him. Everyone turned back at him.

"Is that me? Did I curse you for not being Moothakani? You're the one, you're the one who claimed me as a traitor, a womanizer, a creepy human. You believed that I molested Ponni, you claimed that I killed her. You made the ruckus you dog. Because of your allegation, I lost my life. I lost that woman who is standing behind you. She lost her life believing your false allegation, she lost her entire adulthood just because she loved a man who was accused of molesting her friend. Please don't make a blame game again on me. I'm already living as a rotten piece of shit. Please don't crush me anymore," Marthandan emotionally fumbled and his voice, hands, and everything were shaking.

"Okay, if at all you are honest, what stops you from telling what happened that night? Only we knew that you were the only person who was outside that night. You must have known what happened. What stops you from telling what happened? Tell me a reason, what stops you from telling me what happened? Kaliyan furiously emoted.

"Ponni stopped…It's Ponni who stopped me not to tell," Marthanda spit out from his mind after all those years. Melissa turned at Marthandan and she saw him curiously.

He opened up to say about that night at Dravyapara forest on a new moon day.

*　*　*

That night nineteen years ago, after meeting Melissa and giving the jhumkas to her, he was returning to his home in the middle of that eerie night when Ponni was walking around. He believed that Ponni would have safely crossed the Dravyapara forest, but he was disturbed by the very mild sound of someone running. As it was dense he could hear the sound but was unable to see it in a good picture. First, he hesitated a bit but he was afraid that something might happen to Ponni there, so he went to that path. He cleared away the plants and slowly entered the forest. He heard the sound of someone running mildly at some distance. He reached out there to find none. The forest was playing with him through echo as he couldn't find anyone. He even shouted Ponni's name and he didn't get any reply.

Meanwhile, at quite a distance, Ponni was hiding behind a bush without a sound when she saw someone following her. She was already panicked by the darkness but then the anonymous sound of Marthandan made her even more scared. She closed her eyes and suddenly she was grabbed by a strong hand from behind. She opened her eyes to see only the darkness that surrounded the forest. Her mouth was closed and all she could see was darkness.

She was groped, she was being molested and after a few minutes, she got rid of that hand and fell. She was dragged again, which bruised her body. Ponni tried to take the coconut from her plate and beat him but he escaped and the coconut splashed on the floor into pieces. Immediately she tried to punch that man's face and all she could see was only darkness, not his face. She tried hard only ended up being surrendered to his strength and fell. Her voice was trying so hard to come out of the hands of that man.

The sound from the movement of Arogyapacha plants and Flame Lily gave some hint to Marthandan and he followed that.

Ponni was completely under the control of that man and the darkness helped him to escape from revealing his identity as he was covering his face with the cloth. Ponni saw a predator in front of her in that darkness-filled dense forest. He opened his pants and his hands tightened her mouth even harder. She was unable to breathe and gasped heavily. The man who was feeling her like a predator, took his penis out and suddenly she felt that he is trying to take all over her body. She waited, she stopped crying, she stopped limping, she obeyed him as he caressed her body with his penis, and he slowly came to her upper body.

In a fraction of a second, the blood splashed all over her body as Ponni made a cut on his penis with a sharp piece of coconut strip with a shell that splashed over. She had grabbed that in her hand and waited momentarily to smash it.

The predator was groaning in pain and Ponni stood up and grabbed him and tried to smack him again with the strip but with the penis being cut, the man tried to run away from the place after beating Ponni because he was leaking so much blood that would put him to death. She followed him and ended up losing him in the darkness. She finally found the path took her plate and ran towards it. She reached the Dravyapara to see the lamp lit up there being the only light source. She saw Marthandan running to her by following the sound he heard.

Tears broke out in agony for Ponni after seeing Marthandan and he wasn't sure what had happened to her. He hesitated to go near her since she was not wearing anything. Marthandan closed his eyes and groaned in frustration as he couldn't care about her, he then literally prayed to his deity turned back at her, and took her in his arms. Suddenly Ponni shouted screamed and grabbed his shirt and asked him,

"Chetta, there is a snake all over my body. It was going through my nose, my eyes…and now look at ears, it is coming out…it is coming out…"

Marthandan was confused as he couldn't see anything on her body but Ponni kept on shouting and murmuring that she had been spiraled by a group of snakes all over her body.

She was hallucinating that her fascinating wings were bitten off by the group of snakes. She was horribly traumatized and her body was itching and she felt numbness and cried until she drained out. Marthandan without any idea hugged her made her head rest on his chest and consoled her.

This made Ponni go even more emotional and she cried and told everything that happened a few minutes ago. Marthandan was so angry and got fumed by this and blasted him with words without even knowing who he was. He asked Ponni, how can we find him?

"Chetta, no no no no no no no no, please don't tell this to anyone, especially Kaliyan. He would lose his mind and everything would be shattered, the village needs him, and the tribe needs you both please do not make this an issue."

"How could I just leave someone who made you like this…How can he live?"

"Chetta, I'm Ponni, alle? I did what I was supposed to do, I cut his penis. I guess he would be running with pain. He has to live with that for his entire life. If you want to find that person, let us open every man's lungi. We can have that evidence…"

Marthandan hugged her and consoled and she said,

"Chetta I don't know what these people will think of me being injured in this night. They might think some ghost hit me as if I had sex, don't you think? You're a Plathi alle? Find some medicine here for me, save me, I shouldn't die here. Please make this wound go, Chetta. I'm so scared of being shamed. Please promise me that you won't tell this to anyone especially your soul mate Kaliyan…"

Marthandan promised and went into the forest and came back with the flowers and a mysterious fruit that only a Plathi of the Kani tribe had known for years. He made an extract from his hand made an anti-septic formula and applied it on her body to get rid of the germs and bacteria over the wound. He then carried her on his hands, left her near Isabella's and gave the pooja plate as if it was done without any chaos.

He went back home and called Mullan, who was sleeping in his house. He urged him to give him a drink and the trauma was passed on from Ponni to Marthandan.

He was still being traumatized by that night more than Kaliyan. Everyone who listened to him about that night was frozen and terrified to think of what Ponni went through that night.

Kaliyan was stunned and his eyes rolled down heavily. All he could do was look at Marthandan who kept the promise he made with Ponni for all these years taking the blame on himself and sacrificing his soul mate and his love. The old friends saw each other and did nothing, but they started scolding each other in bad words but this time with more understanding and rights towards each other.

Mani and Valli saw Marthandan and his face changed among them completely, after knowing the whole truth behind that night. Valli apologized to Marthandan and she was crying and thinking of her childhood mentor, Ponni. Joseph and Adina were also amazed by the sacrifice of Marthandan.

After all, Melissa was just staring at Marthandan with all her grievances overflown through her eyes. She was in shock about what she just heard and also there was so much going on in her mind. She seemed to process her entire life within minutes. All she was thinking was the cruelty that was laid upon the mind, the body, and the soul of Ponni.

She went to Marthandan slowly and as everyone was concerned over him, he was thinking that Melissa would do too but instead, she came to him and gave a tight slap over his face and said,

"You're a coward, taking the blame over a promise doesn't make you a hero. You are always a coward and a useless "issue maker", you had changed everything." Melissa started crying and hugged him tightly in front of everyone and Kaliyan turned back and smiled. Mullan who came back from inside after two pegs and listened to him, felt sorry for acting in a way that hurt everyone and he apologized to Kaliyan and also to Valli and he fainted.

"It has vanished, the evidence the proof, the culprit, they have vanished away along with Ponni-ichi," said Mani.

"The only proof was that cut in the penis of that man who did that. But it is hard to pull up the lungies and veshties of every man," Marthandan said slowly.

"It is obvious, the truth must be known. Our entire village is still symbolizing Ponni-ichi as the sign of sin and dirt. If the dirt must be washed away, we need that man. The so-called predator to come out of his mask and accept what has happened…" Valli showed her frustration.

"Chechi, I guess we need not see that. It is not only about the man who did that to her that night. It is all men because we all know what should be inside. Yes, all men do.

Nothing ever changes when a man decides to think from his dick," Adina expressed her thoughts.

"Okay, but what if the man is not alive or not from this place?" Mani asked.

"No, I may know. Ponni needs justice, and I can tell how she will achieve that. Just like Kaliyan said, I know everything about the village right? Yes, I can solve this…I may know who would've done that," Melissa opened up.

Chapter Nineteen

At Kanyakumari, the heat was even higher as Peter was planning to assassinate the couple. He was so upset with Joseph and his act against Peter unknowingly. At his place, he was boozing with his men and he decided to apply the same formula for Adina which they applied for the previous girls of their caste under the same phenomenon. He called Arockiyaraj for the party too.

"It is not only for pride, by now most of our communal members would have known about the issue. If I spare this girl, my entire system will fall out. I have to do this, you should stay away from this," Peter asked Arockiyaraj.

"Peter, I was transferred here just to arrest you! And now you are talking this shit with me? Do you think a cop will allow this?" he said.

"What a man you are! Uhh? I still don't understand you. You were there with me against that lower caste dog that day, but now you're standing against me?"

"Peter, I think I should make one thing clear. I don't want any murder happening inside my circle. Even it is for any and the reason why I stood with you that day. I don't want you to do any damage to the town's peace because of that boy but that doesn't mean that you can do whatever you are willing."

"Hahaha, so finally the ego is winning more than the caste and the communal pride? Right? Okay sir, let me do the wise thing."

Arockiyaraj was not happy with his plan and immediately he wanted to warn Christopher Raj and his family. He went to his house and rang the bell.

Evangeline saw him at their door and was shocked but opened to welcome him in. He warned them to take over their daughter and Joseph soon and get them married and register their marriage so that nobody would be able to interrupt their personal life and they could seek legal assistance without any chaos.

"Christopher Raj, as a cop I'm saying this. You know I may be from the other caste. I never know what I would do if my daughter married a boy from a lower caste. I'm not that generous but I won't let my daughter die for the sake of the pride of the caste," he said to him and he wasn't replying anything.

He then saw Abraham and stared at him and he smiled at him.

Peter was so keen on assassinating both and he called his old friend who helped him a lot in killing the girls of his caste for pride.

"Let that plan be the same, we need to abduct the girl, poison her…cover it as suicide, we must make sure her eyes should be closed and the killing must be curel than what she would've imagined, and she must not be able to see what is happening around her. Then we need to kill her father to make sure the suicide was true and her father killed himself after being shamed by society for marrying her daughter to someone from the other caste… more importantly, her father's death must be done naturally without any trace. Even his family should believe that."

"Okay, where is the girl?" asked his friend.

"That's what we need to find out. She must be in Kerala and two Australians are accompanying her as well. Only her father have heard about that place. But he is not opening up and we must be aware of Arokciyaraj too. He may take a stand against us please ask our men to keep an eye on his daughter at Ramnad."

* * *

In the eve of the Palli festival in Amboori, Father Ben was praying alone in the church as everyone from the church had gone into the streets for the collection. Marthandan just came into the church to call the father along with Kaliyan and Joseph. Everyone greeted the Father.

"Edo, Marthanda, Kaliya, and you…praise the lord," Father greeted.

"Father, I need to take the sacrament of penance," Marthandan said.

"What? Now? What it is for? A moral sin or a venial sin?"

"I don't know father, I just want to have a sacrament of reconciliation. Life has given me a lot and also it has taken a lot from me too. All I can do is to confess the sin that I have done…"

"Okay Marthanda but you haven't baptized. So in what case this will work in the church?"

"I believe in Jesus and I also believe that confessing to you will also make my life better. Isn't that enough to have this? And all of us in our village live dependently on both the religion, alle? Just like both Malayalam and Tamil are blended here?"

"Okay, but I believe you have changed a lot. It seems like the bond between you and Kaliyan is back. After so many long years I'm seeing you two together."

"Yes Father, the things that happened have just changed us. We all need a change in life, right? After all, we are humans, not the Messiah to live without mistakes and sins."

"Ohh, and also Marthandan has learned to talk like a philosopher. The man known for the issues…"

Father giggled, took his bible, and asked him to follow to the small confessional with the small chair inside. He went inside and sat on the chair and asked Kaliyan and Joseph to stay away. He called Marthandan alone to that place. He made him kneel and asked him to start the confession.

"Father, I would like to tell you a story."

Father Ben gave his ears to him and he began.

"Father, years ago I made a mistake. It's more of a sin. I'm still unable to recover from it. The noise and visuals of those times still haunt my brain and my life is entirely ruined by it."

"Okay Marthanda, you can heal from it by confessing it on the foot of The Lord."

"Father…some years ago, exactly when the last time the festival happened in our village, a small hornbill bird was living freely waiting for its wings to come. One day the bird was put to a test to prove something for someone for no reason. It was given the task of fulfilling the dream and the task of the so-called cultured people of our village. The main heads pushed the bird. The bird without the wings went into the darkness of life. The darkness surrounded, then a bird of prey came into the scene, an owl. That owl had wings, huge and strong wings. It came closer to the tiny little wingless hornbill. The darkness made the hornbill go blind, but the owl had the vision clearer than ever. The owl snatched the bird, and the bird fell. The nude bird was seeking help but it couldn't see anything in the darkness. Suddenly, the owl took over its supremacy of power, strength, of masculinity over the poor little hornbill. But the hornbill isn't from a herd of sheep. It is a sole-winning horn bill that dared to snap off half the wings of the owl. The owl was groaning in pain and the owl with broken wings flew away from the darkness. But the hornbill was found by a small mouse which is the troublemaker from the village. The mouse rescued the bird. It thought the bird would survive the owl attack but the village didn't allow it. The manipulation of dirt over the bird began. The cultured civilized animals threw stones at the bird slut shaming the young little bird. No Messiah came at that time to say, "Let him who is without sin among you be the first to throw a stone at her". The poor little bird waited for a Messiah but no one turned up and it turned up to its cat. The most lovable cat that loved the bird more than anyone in the village. The cat wanted to rescue her but the time had gone past everything for the bird. It fell off from the cliff. The cat straight away went to the mouse which was manipulated by some force. The cat and mouse game began. The owl was enjoying everything with the mask of a shepherd. But it made a mistake by trying to snatch another bird. But then the bird wasn't the horn bill without wings. It was an ostrich with heavy wings but unfortunately a dumb ostrich. It had no one to support in her life. The ostrich has seen the broken wing of that owl. The owl doesn't know that the mouse has known about that broken wing, and the poor owl also doesn't know that the ostrich has someone else in the world at the end of the day. It is that mouse. The ostrich had known that the life of the female gender was the same. No one will come and rescue them inside the gate because the gate itself has been doing the sin. The gate with thorns. The owl with horn…Father? Too many metaphors, right?" he finished his story and asked him about it.

His face was sweating and his eyes changed red to hear this story from him. He slowly turned at him and saw him staring. He bit his lips and starred him back and said,

"Eda Marthanda…whom do you think you're? What are you spitting now? Know your limits and shut your mouth, this the church." He was fuming slowly and he turned to his right to see Kaliyan holding himself straight at him with reddish eyes. Suddenly he opened the door of the confessional and saw Joseph standing tall against him.

Father tried to wake up and he was immediately kicked by Joseph up front. He collapsed and fell. Marthandan was still kneeling and he started crying out of pain heavily he cried louder and louder thinking of the life he lost because of that night. He cried and shouted like the church would crumble. He spit out everything from his mind and shed tears that would even sink the church.

"Eda Kaliya…please don't believe him and that bitch, she is the one who…."

Instantly Father Ben was given a blow on the face by Joseph. Immediately Kaliyan came in front of him. Father again fumed.

"Kaliya…you never know my power and authority over this village."

"I know nothing, all I want is, Father Ben with all due respect should come out to the center of the village and accept himself as the pennant and ask for the sacrament of penance in front of our village and should declare what he did that night to my girl. You have a time, and you have your life in your hands. Use it wisely. If you still think you're smarter, then we will show what the men of this tribe, who battle against the wild can do to you. Praise the Lord, tell me back," Kaliyan said to Father.

He took Marthandan up and grabbed the things of Melissa inside the church and all three prayed for a few seconds in front of Jesus and left the church.

Father was still stranded on the ground near the confessional and still thinking about them and he was panicking that his mask was peeled off by these men and he was so confused about what he should do at that moment.

Marthandan and Kaliyan went to Dravypara cliff and saw the clouds slowly fading away from the village and reaching the Agasthiya Malai near the Tamil Nadu border. Those clouds were cleared by the heavy wind. They saw a woman sitting at the edge of the cliff. Marthandan went closer to see Melissa who was sitting there. The wind was blowing heavily at the top of the cliff.

He came close and touched her shoulders. She stood up and his eyes and she understood that he had cried a lot.

"Sorry..." he opened his words with his very shaky voice.

She hugged him tightly and he grabbed her back tightly. The clouds again hazed their love and intimacy even in their forties.

"You know what happened that day when I saw his wounded penis? Please ask me anything you want to know from all these years. I'm sure you would be thinking of that, please ask me. I'll confess to my love..." she asked him.

Marthandan took her away and looked at the clouds again at the dusk and asked.

"I have one thing to ask, please tell me the truth."

Kaliyan turned back at Marthandan. She nodded her head to answer that.

He asked, "How long will you love me?"

Her eyes shrunk by the heavy wind and looked at him closely she grabbed some wind with her both palms then closed it and showed it to him. Immediately she opened her palms and reacted as if the wind from her palm was taken away by the blowing wind.

"As long as this wind exists in this world, I will love you!"

They again hugged and the tribal part of the village Amboori was ready for the Palli festival the next day.

*　*　*

Peter was receiving calls from his fellow caste leaders after knowing about the news of the daughter of a renowned caste man, who had eloped with a guy from a lower caste. He was so worried.

"I will finish her off soon, I will find her, and I will make everything go according to the formula. let me have her identities and belongings."

"Okay, only if you do this, I can speak to the top tier to get you a posting. The party relies only on your caste down south, and you are the only ambassador of your people from us. Please make sure they have the respect and importantly fear you and obey you." a voice spoke over the phone.

Peter cut the call and he seemed very frustrated. He immediately rushed to Adina's and called Christopher Raj.

"I need shawls and some ornaments of your daughter. Those will reach Kothaiyar as evidence, I need to finish her soon."

Evangeline was shocked and started quarreling and Christopher didn't hesitate anything and shut her mouth.

Then he went inside her room after so many years. Abraham was in the other room sitting on a table doing nothing but putting his head down on the table as a sign of not being able to save her sister from this. But none knew that Peter was also planning to kill Christopher to put a complete circle of hate on the caste that Joseph belonged to.

Christopher opened the wardrobe door. He took out her dresses and he saw a childhood picture of her being pasted on the inner part of the door. He opened the inner door again to see a picture of him having Adina as a child. It was taken on the day she got baptized. His hands started to shiver and he couldn't control the emotions of losing his daughter. He was shocked to see her daughter's love towards him and he closed the door he made up his mind again and took the shawl outside the room. Suddenly he was stopped by his wife and she showed something that shook Christopher and also took his mind two decades back.

On the third birthday of Adina, Christopher wasn't able to attend it on time as he couldn't get back home on time. Adina was sad on that day. So after reaching home late at night, she didn't speak to her father. So he decided to buy a gift. He took his bike and went outside but as it was late at night he couldn't find an open shop. Christopher had an idea to go to the beach and grab something that she liked. He went to the beach and was disappointed again to find the shops being closed there as well. He saw the Indian Ocean with an utter disappointment. But suddenly he saw the earth to find some shining under the moonlight. The colored tiny pebbles near the Bhagavathi Amman temple.

He straight away ran in and collected those pebbles grabbed a thread from his file made a chain out of it and rushed back to his house to present her angel the birthday gift. Only then he saw Adina smile and she hugged her father and kissed him on the cheeks.

The same chain was the one his wife was holding in her hands as she found that in Adina's locker.

"Give this one to him as the evidence for our daughter being "made"' suicide by him."

Christopher became anxious and he wasn't able to breathe. He was stuck by the thoughts he just had. The entire life of Adina flashed in front of him. Immediately he collapsed on the floor and started weeping.

Evangeline shouted. Abraham rushed from his room to find his father on the floor and weeping. Christopher steadied himself grabbed that chain in his hands saw Peter and asked him to stay away from his daughter.

"Enough, do whatever you want. Take your caste and everything away from my daughter. She is not the goddess. She is not holding the pride of the caste. She is just my small tiny angel in my hands. I don't want to let her die. I will not let her die. She is my gold. She is my daughter."

Peter smiled at him and cursed him with a few words which made Abraham go against him only ended up getting a slap.

"Christopher...count the days of your daughter. You are underestimating me completely. I will show who I am and what the power of my caste can do." He left the house took his car and moved away. He was receiving so many calls and then he received a call from an unknown number.

Chapter Twenty

The Festival day had finally come in Amboori. The entire village was in completely festive mood. The people from the other places also reached Amboori from the mainland. The mini buses from main land to Neyyar Dam and the Kalakad Wildlife Sanctuary were filled with heads. Many people from the neighboring places and also the Christian tribal communities also reached Amboori.

In the morning, Kaliyan was greeted by Valli and she smiled to show her love towards him. At Mani's, Joseph and Adina were told to get ready before dawn for the morning feast at the church. Alyssa and Brandon, who were just about to recover, badly wanted to attend the festival.

After some recovery, Brandon was able to walk and his wound had slightly gotten better in terms of curing. Alyssa conveyed to Erica about the leaf that they were searching for through the very poor network up the hill. She also found out that someone had been labeling themselves as the Kani tribe's authority providing the resources illegally and selling the patents of the Arogya pacha leaves from the Dravyapara forest.

She also checked with her fellow bio scientists that these particular leaves have been exported largely from the Kerala part of India. But that didn't seem to be Kani's patent. She had a very clear doubt over someone who pretended to be a Kani tribe but not a one. And she also doubted that someone was manipulating Isabella for this.

"Father Ben, it should be…" Joseph said.

"How come?" Alyssa questioned.

"A high possibility. Father is the one who wants this festival to happen, and he also wants to do the Sasthan pooja again. He was afraid that Isabella Ma may choose someone as Moothakani between Kaliyan and Marthandan. So he planned everything to fall right in place making Kaliyan and Marthandan fight for their life. He made sure that they weren't involved in anything good for the tribe and he also manipulated the likes of Isabella Ma and the people of the church. And first of all, he doesn't even belong to the Kani tribe. He is an outsider," Mani who just woke up said to Alyssa.

"What?" Alyssa wondered.

"Yeah, he doesn't belong to the tribe. That is why he always speaks as "you" not "us" when he talks about the activities of the tribe. He came with a missionary long years back and he was stuck with the church. He had been living off with the funds of Roman Catholic all these years."

"Nope, that is how he fooled us. He had known that the Dravyapra had been yielding this Arogya Pacha for years. He had been selling it without anyone's knowledge and he made money out of it also he went on trips then and there to make sure about the illegal dealings. He also claimed himself as a Plathi, who is not a one…"

"Marthandan is the one who is a Plathi. He could have easily caught him. But he ended up being a coward and distracted us all these years," as Mani said this, Adina entered properly dressed up for the occasion.

Meanwhile, at Chithirai Street, Mullan was waking up to the roster sound and he saw Melissa praying at the hall. He couldn't find Marthandan inside the house. He didn't speak to her as she was praying intensively. He came to see a group of people chanting the songs of Jesus. They stopped at the place and asked Mullan,

"Have you seen Melissa?"

Mullan replied none and Melissa from inside heard her name being called out.

"I don't know," said Mullan only to be shocked by Melissa coming out of the house and greeting those people of that group. Mullan wasn't sure what he had to do and didn't know how to react in a way to answer again.

At the church, Father Ben was standing in the same place where he did first aid to his penis after it was injured by Ponni nineteen years ago. He was thinking of everything that happened that night, right from his plan to abduct Ponni alone in the night to make use of the opportunity to molest her. Also, he remembered his intentions towards the poor girl Ponni right from her childhood and he was targeting her to convert to Christianity so that he could pull her into the church as a nun but she wasn't obeying anyone. He recalled the words said by the men the day before to confess and declare that Ponni was a pure soul.

Immediately from his room, he went through the back door and opened it to escape from the village only to find Marthandan sitting across the door with a cup of tea in his hand.

"Good Morning, Enda ponnu Father eh!" he greeted him.

Father didn't know how to react to this embarrassment as he didn't expect this coming. Marthandan stood up and hugged Father greeted him with respect and said,

"No one received their last 'respect' when they were alive. I guess from now on, no one will respect you. You're the blessed among the men, Father."

The center of the village is then ready for the function. The crowd filled the nooks and corners of the village of Amboori from the mainland.

The church's bell was rung by Marthandan. The crowd started coming in, the village was then about to learn the truth from Father Ben.

Both Father and Marthardan were approaching the center of the village. All the others include Melissa, Kaliyan, Joseph, Adina, Mullan, Valli, Mani, Alyssa, and Brandon. He asked Father to start confessing. He started.

"To the son of God, to the Almighty."

"Okay, we have had enough of your almighties." Kaliyan stopped him.

"Edo Kaliyaa, let him do his gimmicks for one last time," Marthandan interrupted and as he was smiling at

Kaliyan he instantly changed his face and turned back at the Father furiously and said,

"Enda Ponnu Father-eh, start it."

Father Ben who was scared of their moves instantly opened his mouth.

"Ponni isn't dirty. She isn't unholy, she isn't unholy."

Meanwhile as the sun slowly reaching the west, Isabella was taken on shoulders by a group of men to the center of the village. Everyone then was unable to listen to Father clearly as the crowd focused on Isabella Ma coming into the meeting. She saw Melissa and she gave a look at Isabella which only Melissa would have known to understand.

"Isabella ma, Isabella ma, I must confess. Ponni isn't dirty…Ponni isn't unholy…she is a sign of holiness," Father expressed his views and cried at her.

"Who is Ponni?" asked Isabella from the top of the shoulders of two men.

"Yes…Who is Ponni?" asked a voice from the crowd.

Another voice popped to ask the same, "Who is Ponni? We don't remember…"

"I remember now. Ponni is the goddess that went inside the Dravyapara years ago. Do you guys remember the story of sow and reap on a day that happened at Dravyapara. The nude god was seen by one of the men from the village. At that moment the goddess went inside and never came back. Isn't she the one you guys are talking about?" Isabella ma told.

"Yeah my Ponni is the goddess but we are all humans and acted in a way to search for the holiness of our goddess…right?" Kaliyan said.

Another voice from the crowd said, "What are you even talking about? We people are cultured to see a woman as a goddess."

"But we never see them as a woman. We never care about their rights. We never think about their proper human feelings. We always had seen them as a sign of purity and the sign of holiness and the symbol of pride, to keep the pride in the women," Kaliyan replied to the crowd.

"Ohh, I didn't know that. By the way, why Father Ben is now crying in front of the village?" asked Isabella.

Marthandan didn't hesitate a bit and slapped Father in front of the crowd and asked him to confess more and said,

"Eda…Father eh…where did all the money come from? What are all the plans you made to stop him from being the Moothakani? Confess everything now."

"Ponni is a pure and holy woman. She was brutely molested by our village. That night I was the one who followed Ponni when she was doing the Sasthan pooja. I was always fond of her but due to her family, she never came to church and also never listened to me. So I saw the chance and I took it but she was brave. She cut my penis into almost half and I was bleeding which could have made the animals chase me sensing the blood. So I decided to get back and I got some random leaves from the Dravyapara. Those leaves stopped my bleeding and in the morning my skin started to heal. But I didn't know the leaf's name. So

I decided to learn it from the Plathi. It was Marthandan but he stopped telling it so I offered a drink to Mullan and boozed Marthandan indirectly. I asked him about the leaves and their benefits. He told me everything while boozing. He didn't even know that he told me. I decided to earn a patent for that leaf but I was afraid that Kaliyan becoming Moothakani would create problems for me. I was planning to stop that but fate played differently. Both Kaliyan and Marthandan were split and they started fighting for it. I made use of that opportunity. I started selling Arogyapacha but I couldn't earn a patent because of not being one of the tribes. So I decided to be a one using the Palli festival without the Moothakani. Everything was going well until these Australians came onto the scene. They found out the Arogya Pacha and its dealers."

He was slapped by Mullan from the back, for using him as a coin to make Marthandan drunk.

Father saw Melissa and stared at her and only ended up having a wack from Marthandan. The crowd was so silent and some were in shock after their beloved Father Ben broke the hard truth about him.

Kaliyan and Marthandan took Isabella down made her sit in front of the crowd and asked, "What should we do now?"

Isabella looked up to the sky and saw the clouds moving.

"What should I do my lords? Do I need to take the forgiveness card just like you two said or else should I punish him for the sins he committed?"

Everyone looked into the eyes of Isabella while she was seeking inspiration from Lord Krishna and Messiah Jesus Christ.

Suddenly she said, "Let us start the Palli festival. People have gathered and the festival should begin. We should not make them stranded. Let him stay at the church for a day and let the Gods decide his fate. Let the Palli festival start."

As she asked them to start it, the musical instruments at the church started the buzz and the children and the young people started rushing to the church. Kaliyan and Marthandan took him to the church locked him in his room and made Mullan his guard.

Melissa took over the church and she started the blessing prayer in the evening. Adina, Joseph, Mani, Alyssa, Brandon, and Valli were together in the church. A special feast was also arranged nearby and the cooking was also happening in the shed nearby.

Both Marthandan and Kaliyan were roaming and watching out the festivals as they were then together and they believed that being united could make them better and also for the village.

Marthandan took over the northern half of the church and Kaliyan took care of the Southern part of the church. Meanwhile, inside the room, Mullan was having a drink and he often slapped Father Ben, saying,

"Because I'm bored."

At the eastern part of the church, the young boys from the village burst a cracker and Marthandan came running in and stopped them not to as the wild animals could come into the village because of the fire light and the sound.

Kaliyan also rushed from the south to stop the boys but as they were doing that they heard a monumental sound from the west of the church as a sky-high cracker was lit up in the air and it created a massive light and made the church dusk turn into a day for few seconds.

Melissa from inside the church rushed out and said,

"Wild animals may come."

Joseph, Adina, Alyssa, Brandon, and Mani also came out to see.

Both Marthandan and Kaliyan went to the west and stopped the boys and watered the crackers.

Then, they heard the other sound. The sound of a car with a heavy headlight flashing and horning.

Peter Durai got out of the car. Adina and Joseph were shocked to see him. Peter saw the church and he noted Adina, then he smiled and tapped at the banet of his car.

"Fatherrrrrrr...." Peter shouted.

Meanwhile, Father from the inside got rid of drunken Mullan and ran outside the church and rushed to see Peter. It was him who called Peter Durai when he was leaving Adina's house and he informed Peter about Joseph and Adina as he was the one who helped Marthandan and Kaliyan to find out the truth.

Palli was packed by the people and the clash between good and evil was just about to begin.

Chapter Twenty One

Adina and Joseph were panicking at the church steps and no one from the village had known about Peter except Father Ben. Father rushed to him for rescue and Peter saw Adina hiding behind Joseph. Marthandan and Kaliyan were rushing to the spot to see Melissa slowly coming down the steps of the church.

Peter asked his men to take care of Father and he approached Adina. Joseph was adjusting his sleeves and waited for Peter to come to her who was hiding behind her. Kaliyan saw Peter approaching Adina and he got furious and ran in to stop him. Peter fumingly tried to grab Adina's hand but his hand was grabbed by an external hand that had a lightened candle in it and its base's wax was melting down. It was placed on Peter's hand strongly. Joseph was shocked to see and Kaliyan slowed down his run seeing Melissa doing the job.

Peter was heavily groaning in pain but still, he tackled himself and tried to attack Joseph. He rolled his sleeves up again. Peter was stopped by another hand. This time it was Marthandan.

He slapped him continuously with both hands and Peter was almost pushed to the state of Trance. He relieved himself and tried to slap him back but his head was immediately covered by Mullan's lungi and he pushed him to kneel and he punched his face, leaving Marthandan again.

Kaliyan called Marthandan and said,

"Only a few morons. I don't want our Palli festival to get interrupted because of these germs. Let that happen. Let us finish them off in our way."

Marthandan immediately rushed to Peter's vehicle and stood up on it. Father Ben who was ready to escape saw Marthandan and planned to run away from the car. But he was grabbed by Marthandan and he gave some tight slaps to him in his way.

The rally of village Christians with Jesus Christ's statue was about to reach back to the church after wandering the tribal village and the Amboori mainland.

Kaliyan didn't want the village to know about the crisis. So he wanted Marthandan to stop slapping the Father but suddenly Father escaped him and ran into the church again. Melissa followed him and Father, groaning in pain, fell at the feet of Isabella who was made to sit in a chair, wearing a golden color saree wrapped over a foil shawl she was given a bottle of water in her hand and her head was covered by a crown-like hat which Holy Mother Mary used to wear. He started to cry at the feet of Isabella Ma and asked her to forgive him for what he did.

Marthandan, Kaliyan, Valli, Joseph, Adina, and Mani came into the church following them.

Outside, as the rally was coming in, he saw a two-wheeler coming and he was shocked to see Arockiyaraj.

He followed the phone signal of Peter and found out the place. Peter was relieved to see Arockiyaraj as the cop would save him.

Peter also came in and asked Father not to beg her.

"Hey, stop crying and I'm going to screw everyone. These bullshit tribes have no civilization and they have no sense at all. We have a cop with us, this place will be doomed…"

Arockiyaraj entered the church and everyone looked at him differently as they rarely see a cop over the tribal village and that too he arrived with the warrant paper.

Marthandan and Kaliyan were getting ready to knock him off as they didn't like the cops either. Peter was quarreling and cursing at Joseph and he decided to snap his head right in front of Adina.

"Come on, you lower caste dog. You never had any right to even stand in front of me," Peter quarreled heavily and asked Arockiyaraj to take Joseph down.

Immediately Marthandan and Kaliyan jumped over the benches and approached Arockiyaraj but they stopped suddenly. Adina, Mani, Valli, Joseph, and everyone looked shocked. Peter who was smiling with all his evilness that outcame at that moment suddenly stopped as Arockciyaraj grabbed the hands of Peter firmly and locked it with the handcuff.

Arockiyaraj smiled at Joseph and he smiled back at him as well. It was his plan.

"Vadaa Petre-uh" said Arockiyaraj. Peter had no clue what happened and he said,

"Arockiyaraj…what are you even doing? Have you forgotten your daughter?"

He immediately slapped Peter gave him a tight stare and said,

"My daughter is well, safe and good, don't worry about her, please worry about your men who abducted my daughter."

Everything that Peter planned was flashing in his mind. Right from a few days ago he threatened Arockiyaraj about his daughter in Ramnad. The way he behaved after that with Joseph made him think that he might also be an upper caste who felt proud of his birth and thought about her daughter loving a person from another caste but it wasn't the case. He was threatened using his daughter as he would abduct her and manipulate Arockiyaraj. He was helpless and he acted in a way that Peter wanted him to react with his bail and also with Joseph.

Arockiyaraj confessed to Joseph that after he left home without his shoes, he was the one who asked him to stay at the tribal village with the Australians and allowed Peter to track them. Arockiyaraj had known that Peter would kidnap his daughter. So he made a plan to get rid of her and rescued her using his friends from Ramnad and Rameswaram then he grabbed the evidence against Peter and informed Joseph about it and hit the village.

Joseph's smile told the truth to Adina and she was so happy about Peter being arrested with the proper evidence.

Peter was seeing everything furiously and without knowing what would have happened at Ramnad but suddenly Arockiyaraj received a call.

"Assalamu Alaikum…Latif bhai, much thanks for the timely help, I will never forget this."

A man spoke over the phone, "Walaikum Assalam… Hahaha, there is nothing in the world called "help" sir. It's all because of what we did and what we need. Ramnad is waiting for you. Come back sooner."

"Sure bhai…" He cut the call and said to Peter,

"I have few friends from Ramnaad and Rameswaram and you have completely miscalculated what I was doing at Rameswaram."

Peter was fuming within himself and he was terrified with himself. He dragged down Father Ben who called him, but he who held the legs of Isabella pulled her as well made her fall as well.

Isabella's head hit the ground and she opened her mouth. Melissa and Valli rushed towards Isabella while Marthandan and Kaliyan were grabbing Peter along with Arockiyaraj.

Father Ben tried to go away from the scene but he was trapped by Joseph who pulled his legs when he tried to jump over the benches. Arockiyaraj tried to catch him.

Peter who was on the floor with the handcuff made use of this diversion from Arockiyaraj, took out the gun from his pocket pushed him down, and tried to trigger the gun.

When everyone struck at their places Father Ben was climbing up slowly, as he might escape from the place.

As Peter was acting psychic, the entire church went calm and silent. Isabella who fell near the lamp of the church which was filled with melted wax oil candles, saw Father Ben closely. She remembered every evil thing he did to him all these years and also she remembered the face of Ponni. She suddenly pushed the lamp and the wax splashed all over the floor getting splashed in the eyes of Peter and he triggered the gunshot Father Ben on his knees. He was shouting in pain as the rally simultaneously entered the church with the heavy fireworks around the church that synced with the sound of a gun fired there. Isabella took back the crown that she lost when she fell placed it on her head proudly and sat like the holy chosen one from women.

The rally entered the church. The Jesus statue was taken into the church as there was only Isabella Ma sitting on the chair with a crown on her head with the Holy Mother Mary's makeover. The statue was kept and asked Isabella about it and she murmured.

"Dear son, what should I do to the King of Sins?"

The Jesus statue was given to her hand and it was taken to the main arena and was kept at the place.

Peter's eyes and mouth were covered and he was taken by Arockiyaraj to the place where his van was parked along with his Police team from Kerala and Tamil Nadu.

Arockiyaraj thanked Marthandan and Kaliyan for their help and went to Joseph.

"You are brave and your voice needs to be told louder. It should be the voice of the oppressed."

"Sir, I didn't know to voice for the people. I'm not even a guy who wakes up early in the morning. I don't live a honorable life or even a political life but society pushes the people like me to be political. Society made us think whatever we do is political and we must breach the benchmark at least by a nice distance to achieve what others can achieve at their fullest. I don't want to live a political life, I'm a common man I can live within my world," Joseph replied.

"Joseph, even if you try to evade from the politics, politics will chase you until the last breath of yours. Life is always political and love shouldn't be but to live a life politically well, you need to find love in politics."

"I will try sir…" said Joseph and Arockiyaraj left the place.

He took Peter and started moving away from the church.

Before he saw Father Ben, he looked at Marthandan with a curious look about what they were going to do to them.

"It's up to our deity, Isabella ma," said Kaliyan. Arockiyaraj left the place along with Peter.

Marthandan and Kaliyan untied the hands of Father Ben who was made to sit in the backyard of the church. Meanwhile, Valli took Isabella ma out of the church and took her to the backyard.

"Over to you…" said, Marthandan.

Isabella saw the face of Father Ben and she looked above and saw the sky.

"Lord Krishna…No Jesus Christ…No it's Krishna I guess. But Christ said the same right?"

"For God's sake, please tell us what they said," shouted Mani.

"To forgive the sinner, to forgive the sins of the sinner, you need to be God. They are the God…" said Isabella Ma.

Everyone looked at each other.

"Let the Moothakanis's take him to our deity's Dravyapara. Let our deity take care of him."

She moved slowly and Valli took care of her.

Both Marthandan and Kaliyan took Father Ben on their shoulders and went to Dravyapara on the same night. They dropped him down and it was pitch black that was devoted to that place every night. Marthandan took out a bundle of crackers from his dhoti and gave it to Father Ben whose mouth was gagged up with a cloth. He asked Kaliyan to take out the cloth.

"Eda..Eda..Enda ponnu Marthanda…Kaliyaa…please spare me a chance to live. It is unfortunate that night. Ponni wasn't co-operating. If she had cooperated with me, things would have been different. Please, please understand the situation. I'm not even from your tribe. You cannot expect me to live like you all and Marthanda. Your girl Melissa, you should know what happened between us."

Suddenly Marthandan kicked him in the shoulders and went to him

"I may or may not know what happened. But I have already decided what to do to you. That is already a virtue of cruelty to me. Please do not confess anything about Melissa and get my cruelty upgraded," he pushed him tied the cracker near him, and decided to fire it with the hands of Kaliyan so the wild animal would have a good supper. He gave the matchbox to Kaliyan and when he was about to light up that,

"Edo…Kaliyaa please stop it, you guys saw Peter, right? He was taken by that cop. He may not be killed. He will live and realize the mistake he made. Please give me a chance to live, please Kaliyaaa, I beg you –."

Kaliyan's face turned and his mind flashed the heavy flaps of wings from the hornbill with the face of his Ponni smiling and telling,

"When will I fly across this? I just wanted to live."

Kaliyan closed his eyes and did the rest. He lit up the fireworks.

Chapter Twenty Two

The next morning at the Amboori tribal village, the aftermath of the festival day began slowly along with the sun rising in the east. Isabella was cleaned by Valli and she was given the food and handed her over to Mani. She left the place and came back to Aavani Street at Kaliyan's. She kissed the little girl Cinderella also known as Ponni and got ready for school. Kaliyan was wiping his bike and Ponni was about to get on the bike. Kaliyan said,

"Shall we go to Sasthan temple?"

They went to Sasthan temple and the crowd gathered at the temple. The church was taken over by Melissa and she controlled the church also she announced the death news of Father Ben who was accidentally eaten by a bear or wolf at Dravyapara during his night walk along the slope from which they only found some pieces of his body. Some people in the crowd knew what would have happened and some murmured that Ponni's spirit would have killed Father as he did the sins towards her.

Melissa conducted a silent prayer for the passing away of Father Ben.

"Let his soul rest in the feet of God who can purify the dirt and unholy into pure and holy." The crowd slowly started to disperse but Joseph, Adina along with Alyssa and Brandon stood there with their bags.

Marthandan in his bike came later with two more bags of Brandon and gave it to them.

Alyssa opened her laptop and called Valli. She showed the module of the newly to be renovated building of the Kanikar welfare school that was going to be renovated soon from her NGO with the help of the Kerala Government. She took out the bag which had a bunch of Arogya Pacha leaves whose patent should be in the name of Plathi, who was Marthandan. She showed the documents that were ready to gain the full patent in the name of Kanikar welfare, with the "Plathi" Marthandan under the "Moothakani" Kaliyan. Melissa saw everything and smiled at Alyssa and said,

"Thank you for being the chosen holy goddess for our village."

"Melissa, no one is the goddess, If you see someone as the goddess, the rest of the people may or may not be seen as a devil. So let's eradicate this goddesss system. Let us all be poor and pitty humans. Not only my Erica, but every person who is suffering from cancer and the chemos would also be so grateful for this entire Kanikar tribe and your ancestors, especially to the generations of the Plathi," Alyssa said and smiled at everyone.

Brandon said,

"Not only Erica, but every woman who was surrendered under the name of culture, caste, and religion is having cervical cancer. People like Father Ben and Peter are the killing cells. They always care about the middle part of the cervix. One sees the pleasure and wants to own the vagina and the other one sees the pride and their caste's holiness in the vagina, there is nothing different between cancer and these men regarding the vaginas. People are fighting within themselves in the name of castes religion and blah blah blah. You can take this village as an example. You saw Kaliyan and Marthandan fighting between themselves, and someone above them used their rift as a luxury to live better. But they united and eradicated the rust. That's what happening everywhere. We people should not anyone from above apply the divide-and-rule policy again. Arockiyaraj was a gem. He never allowed that. We need more Arockiyarajs than Josephs. I hope you all get it."

"Without Mani, we wouldn't have got a chance to see these gems in our life. Where is he?"

"He will be at Isabella Ma's. You can call him and inform him," said Valli.

By the time she told this, Mani came running in to send off them.

"Thank you," said Adina.

"You will be missed," said Melissa.

"If everything goes right, we will set up our honeymoon here," said Joseph.

Everyone smiled and Alyssa, Brandon Joseph, and Adina moved from the village towards the Amboori mainland with Mani.

Marthandan turned and took back the bike. But he saw Melissa still looking at him from the rear mirror. He came back to her and started the conversation.

"So?"

"So?"

"Yes."

"Yes."

"Issues are over with me," said Marthandan.

"I know," she said.

"I was waiting all these years…"

"I know…"

"I knew you wouldn't have forgotten me"

"I know…"

"Marthandan only knows Melissa…"

"I know."

"I literally missed you,

From the sun's rays to the blue moons, now and then I missed you,

From the water drops to the rain falls, I missed you,

I missed only you."

"I know," she said.

"I always loved you."

"I know."

"I never did anything."

"I know," she said.

"Then what stops you from getting back to me?"

"Marthanda… you deserve better. I have lost myself. For many days I have lost myself. I lost how I loved you. I forgot how to be with you. I forgot how to love a person. I forgot how to be intimate with a person. I had forgotten everything that love life needs. For several years I devoted myself to a force I have never seen. I think I've forgotten myself Marthanda."

"But Melissa, you haven't forgotten me? It is a blessing in disguise for us Melissa. We are not resuming in our mid-forties. We are starting our lives in mid-forties. Not many people will have this fortune."

Melissa went silent and looked at him, and noted his pocket.

He still had that letter in his pocket with the petals of a rose without thorns at that time.

"Rose without a thorn is always safe. That's why."

Melissa took out the letter and smiled, then saw the rose without a thorn and said,

"Roses are beautiful aren't they? It always needs a thorn to live safely."

Marthandan got back his innocent blinking face and Melissa slowly pulled his shirt and hugged him tightly. The blossoms of Amboori village bloomed with the aroma of love spread across the Western Ghats.

*** 3 MONTHS LATER ***

In Brisbane, Australia, Erica was slowly recovering from the cancer and her reports had improved a lot compared to previous months along with the chemotherapy and the Arogya Pacha treatment. Alyssa kissed Erica on the lips and she fed her food Brandon was getting back home in the car with the packs of Arogya Pacha from the "Kanikar Medicinal Pharms" owned by them in the patent name of "Plathi" Marthandan from Amboori, Thiruvananthapuram district, Kerala state, India. She also written a thesis about the oncology treatment among children mentioning the little girl Parvathy she saw at Kanyakumari.

❊ ❊ ❊

At Amboori, the district collector of Thiruvananthapuram inaugurated the "Ponni Kanikar Welfare School, Amboori tribal village" in front of Isabella Ma. The collector took the hands of Isabella Ma and made her cut the ribbon of the school. The collector also inaugurated the "Ponni's Woman Welfare Trust of Kanikars" which would provide free medicines and sanitary pads for women and also would serve as the counseling center for women. The trust's motto is also to bring the women out of the house who were stuck because of their cultural, communal, and religious beliefs.

Valli was given a permanent government job as a teacher at the school and also she was accompanied by two more teachers from Idukki. Kaliyan was working hard as the "Moothakani" to bring the bus road service to Amboori tribal village as the mini busses were stopped only upto the mainland. Kaliyan and Valli were yet to be married because they had no time to fix the marriage as they were busy engaged in social work. Mani was taking care of the official works of the trusts and the export of medicines from the village.

Marthandan was looking after the crops and yields of medicinal plants from Dravyapara and other parts of the Amboori and he also shared the patent money entirely with the Kanikar welfare trust. Mullan who was owing a honey parlor and he used to extract the wild natural honey of Kanikars who went to the forest and brought the money back home.

Melissa was appointed as the trustee of the independent church of Amboori and she took care of all the devotees and functions. She also took the pledge that the Sasthan festival would happen every year to show gratitude towards the Vettikadu Pei and Vadamala bootham beyond Dravyapara but the nude walk phenomenon and the chosen one practice had been eradicated. She believed that the practice of the Church was so important as Jesus Christ is one of the prominent icons in bringing people together with respect to peace and love. They were also building a new hut near Isabella Ma's and Melissa was then two months pregnant.

At Cape Comorin, Pallam Beach was about to see another beautiful sunset. Joseph and Adina were sitting in their favorite place where they used to hang out before. She was resting her head on his shoulders and both were waiting for the sun to set.

"Babe," she called him.

"Hmm?"

"When was the last time we sat like this together without any obstacles in our life?"

"Last time? Have you gone mad? This is the first time," he said.

She smiled and asked, "Shall I ask you one thing?"

Suddenly he received a call from his mom and he spoke over the phone.

"Joseph, Zayan is home. He wants me to make a fish curry. He got addicted to my fish curry when I was staying at their house. Please come soon and ask Adina to come as well. I just bought the fish…"

"Ma, will come back sooner, and ask him to eat first and please request him to leave some fries for us," he cut the phone and looked at her. Then she received a call from Abraham.

"Ma, Adina…this is daddy speaking."

"Yeah, paa."

"We are going out to purchase the engagement outfit for you. Can you ask Joseph's mother to accompany us? Maybe she can select better."

"Ahhh, paa I think his mother is busy cooking a fish curry and she wants me to have dinner there so she can't come."

"So you're not coming as well?"

"Pa…"

"Adina, I swear in the name of god. You should accept whatever dress I select for you. You shouldn't pull a nerve with me then."

"Paa, whatever is fine with me."

"Okay, then what's Joseph's shirt si…." Abraham immediately grabbed the phone and asked his dad to go. Abraham took the phone alone and spoke to Adina.

"Adina, there is an issue…" her face changed and she put the phone on speaker.

"Yes tell me."

"Adina, listen carefully, have you seen the news? Peter Durai escaped from the cops on his way to court. You know whom will he target first. I'm so scared of it. Please get back home along with him as soon as possible. Call Arockiyaraj sir immediately," having said that Abraham cut the call.

Joseph's face was sweating and he started to check everyone on the beach and also Adina's face changed as well and she suspected each and every one on the beach including the vendor of the snack. He called Arockiyaraj and said,

"Sir, what is even happening?"

"Stay calm, where are you?"

"Pallam beach…"

"I'll come there."

Arockiyaraj came to the beach and greeted Joseph and Adina. Joseph was furiously coming at Arockiyaraj and said,

"Sir, what is even happening? How come he escaped? He is a cold-blooded murderer. We did all the efforts for you to catch him. Now how could have he escaped?"

"Listen to me. I'll tell you how he escaped."

Arockiyaraj took them back to the day of the Palli festival. After he left the church, Marthandan and Kaliyan took Father Ben to Dravyapara to give the cracker treatment for him. At that time, Father Ben was pleading to Kaliyan to leave him by saying,

"Edo…Kaliyaa please stop it, you guys saw Peter, right? He was taken by that cop, he may not be killed, but he will live and realize the mistake he made, please give me a chance to live, please Kaliyaaa, I beg you…" suddenly a torchlight struck Father Ben's face.

It was Arockiyaraj who came with Peter whose mouth was wrapped up with a cloth same as Father Ben. Peter's eyes were closed with the hot wax and he couldn't see what was going around him. Arockiyaraj pulled out the cloth from his mouth and Peter started shouting.

"Where am I? Where am I? Where am I?"

"Hell…" answered Arockiyaraj.

"Yes, Marthandan and Kaliyan, can you guys do a favor? I don't want cancer cells to spread even inside the jail or even in my place. Will your deity also take him away?"

Both Marthandan and Kaliyan looked at Arockiyaraj and he smiled at them and said,

"Let me take care of that bullet. You two please take care of them."

After listening to his voice he started fuming and the only thing he listened to was the cracker sound that was lit by Kaliyan and all Peter could hear was the footsteps of some people. He was tied along with Father Ben who was unable to move because of the bullet that pieced through his knee when Peter fired at church. Peter could drag Father Ben away as his eyes were shut with wax and he couldn't see anything at all.

Peter tried to move away from the forest for one last time and failed again only crying heavily and the cry matched the howling of some animals. He shouted louder and louder only to be silenced by the breathing sound of some animal to his left. Peter didn't know what that animal was and he remained silent by sensing that but Father shouted suddenly at the pain in his knee and that wolf started biting both of them. Then the other wild animals followed the wolf.

Peter tried hard to open his eyes full of wax but he couldn't see anything but the dark, suddenly he saw a light the brightest of all lights from the Dravyapara rock. Peter couldn't see anything and he forgot that he lost his vision few hours ago, he battled hard to see the light but he couldn't see anything. The traumatized mind of Peter stated visualizing through the light. The gate of Dravyapara opened after centuries and nude woman coming out of the rock and she stood against both the men, she was as gigantic as the hill and as bright as a shining star, the nude woman came in front of both the men and bombarded with a heavy noise, Peter was groaning in pain and he closed his ears with that sound and he suddenly again heard the noise of Father Ben shouting and the sound of the splashing of some gold coins from the pot in the hands of that nude woman, the chosen goddess. Immediately, the lights went off and the silence emerged as Father Ben's noise was cut off and then Peter's neck and head were snatched and eaten by the animals and so did Father Ben's.

Joseph and Adina were shocked to see Arockiyaraj's face and Joseph asked,

"Sir, but what about all these days? You were producing him in the court?"

"Did you see him? Didn't you think why his face was covered with the black cover? Haha as long as you people won't think, we will have all these loops to solve the unwanted cells that are growing in society. The escaped dead man will be encountered sooner and I will be transferred from here much sooner too. As said, everyone's life is a statement. When we live, it's our choice to make the statement a good one or the evil one. I have heard from your father that you two got engaged now. Congrats, have a great political life ahead."

Both Joseph and Adina were still in shock, and Arockiyaraj said,

"Hello, smile guys smile, no matter what, keep smiling. Go and enjoy the view. It's time, bye." Arockiyaraj took his car and left the beach.

Joseph and Adina came back to their place and looked at the waves one by one again. The Indian Ocean never stopped telling stories through the waves. She got back her head on Joseph's shoulder and started looking at the ocean again. The orange sunset was getting ready to be served. Joseph again compared the wavy hair of Adina with the waves that were appearing every second. Her face glowed in the orange sunset. The ocean water glittered like gold.

The wind blew heavily hitting their ears. The final rays of the day from the sun sparkled over the ocean along the tides.

Joseph turned to Adina

"Babe..."

"Hmm...?"

"You wanted to ask something right?"

"Hmm...!"

"Yes...?"

Adina held his arms tighter. She adjusted her head and made it rest of his shoulder better and saw the waves again. She asked.

"Can we be together forever?"

Acknowledgements

I thank my mom, Vee Thamil, for her love and support throughout this book's journey, right from the idea to execution. Her love is the only thing that has been constantly making me dream and accomplish things with courage.

To Harsha to whom I should be incredibly grateful for helping me in setting the plot and narration of the story; without her involvement and encouragement, this wouldn't have been possible.

To Fayiza, for providing me some wonderful insights from the world of women, which helped me a lot to conclude this story, and special thanks for answering a million of my dumb questions.

To Stephy, for being so generous in taking care of the language department of this book; her enthusiasm towards this book enhanced the language of English to another level.

To Hassain, for providing me the endless support, and also for being one of my frontline supporters before starting this book, just like every time. To Abby, Anbu, Aakash, and Supraja for being there for me whenever I needed a pause or emotional support throughout this journey.

I miss my dad, thatha, and ammachi, who are not with me now, but their teachings and memories will be the best gifts of my life.

These acknowledgements would not be complete, of course, without a mention of my beloved students; their zest towards me and my works have been driving me along. Thanks to my colleagues for a supportive environment and my publishing team for making my book attain its shape.

About The Author

Porchezhian, known by his pen name Porches, is an emerging literary voice whose creativity and passion for storytelling resonate deeply within each of his works. From a rich educational background with graduation in Mechanical Engineering and Masters in Advanced Psychology, Porches brings a unique perspective to his writing, weaving intricate narratives that explore the complexities of love, life and beautiful human emotions.

His debut novel, *The Eternal Chaos of Love (2022)*, captivated readers and garnered him the Best Debut Novel award at the Indian Glory Awards in Dubai (2023). Porches' literary journey also includes a collection of published short stories, namely *It was my fault (2021)* and *The First Night (2022),* featured in anthologies such as *The Minds Scribble* and *Detour,* respectively, as well as a series of online stories such as *Psalm of Murder (2020)* and *A String of Musings (2024),* which showcase his versatility as a writer.

An accomplished poet, he published four poems, namely *Come along; as long as you can, Life in a Nutshell, PostScript (PS),* and *Uncanny Thoughts* in the anthology called *Sound of the Soul (2023),* and a poem *I'll name every flower after you* in the anthology called *Amare Memoria (2023),* kind of poems that delve into the depths of human experience through evocative verse. He received numerous accolades, including the Pages of Perfection award at the Cherry Book Awards in Bangalore (2023), recognition as the Most Aspiring Young Writer at the True Awards in Jaipur (2023), and the Best Fiction Book Award at The Indian Awaz's Author Awards in Guwahati (2024).

Beyond his literary pursuits, Porches is dedicated to nurturing the next generation of writers. He currently serves as a Creative Content Writing Trainer at STEP, The Hindu Group in Chennai, and as a personality development and writing skills trainer at various arts colleges.

Known for his humility, compassion, and relentless work ethic, Porches pours his heart into every piece he crafts. With a commitment to authenticity and creativity, he invites readers to join him on a journey through the landscapes of his imagination, where every story is a testament to the beauty of human connection.

He can be reached at,

porcheswrites@gmail.com,

www.instagram.com/@_porches_,

www.facebook.com/Porches,

sporches.wordpress.com.